YOU'RE ON

A PRACTICAL COURSE IN DRAMA AND THEATRE ARTS

Rob Galbraith

Longman Cheshire

Longman Cheshire Pty Limited
Longman House
Kings Gardens
95 Coventry Street
Melbourne 3205 Australia

Offices in Sydney, Brisbane, Adelaide
and Perth. Associated companies, branches,
and representatives throughout the world.

Copyright © Longman Cheshire Pty Ltd 1991
First published 1991
Reprinted 1992 (twice)

All rights reserved. Except under the conditions described
in the Copyright Act 1968 of Australia and subsequent
amendments, no part of this publication may be reproduced,
stored in a retrieval system, or transmitted in any form
or by any means, electronic, mechanical, photocopying,
recording, or otherwise, without the prior permission of
the copyright owner.

Designed by Mark Davis
Set in 10/12 Bembo
Produced by Longman Cheshire Pty Ltd
Printed in Malaysia — LWP

National Library of Australia
Cataloguing-in-Publication data

Galbraith, Rob.
    You're on: a practical course in drama and theatre arts.
    ISBN 0 582 86991 9.

    1. Drama in education. 2. Theater. I. Title.
792

To understand the meaning of life,
man invented theatre
—*Joseph Joubert*
(1754–1829)

Youth is the time to go flashing from one
end of the world to the other . . . to hear
the chimes at midnight . . . and wait all day
in the theatre to applaud
—*Robert Louis Stevenson*
(1850–94)

ACKNOWLEDGEMENTS

Special thanks to:

Melbourne Theatre Company, and especially to Peter Matheson and Libby Ross
The Performing Arts Museum, and especially to Sally Dawes and Janine Barrand
The Victorian Arts Centre, and especially to Nedjeljka Viduka
The Victorian College of the Arts School of Dance
The Australian Ballet
Hocking and Woods
Handspan Theatre
Strand Electric
Adelaide Arts Festival
Graeme Base
Philip Lethlean
Hugh Colman
Greg Temple
Richard Jeziorny
Peter Ralph

For permission to reproduce photographs we should like to thank the following: Adelaide Festival Centre, page 144; The Herald and Weekly Times Ltd, page 133, Hocking and Woods, page 136, Melbourne Theatre Company, pages 54, 71, 74, 75, 78, 79, 82, 83, 87, 94, 109, 111, 153; New York Public Library Performing Arts Research Centre, pages 152, 157; Performing Arts Museum, Victorian Arts Centre, pages 27, 90, 92, 127, 131, 136, State Theatre Company of South Australia, page 77; Victoria and Albert Museum, London, pages 149, 151, 158, Yale University Theatrical Prints Collection, page 150.

CONTENTS

Acknowledgments *iv*
Introduction *vii*

I In Role 1

1 A note to teachers 3
Workshopping *3*
Physicalisation *5*
A format example *5*

2 From workshop to stage 12
Characters (the who) *12*
Themes (the what) *15*
Structure (the how) *17*
Scenes and settings (the where) *18*
Time (the when) *18*
Motivation (the why) *19*
Development (the what-then) *20*
Some approaches to script *21*

3 Creating a role 24
The value of role-play *24*
Methods of creating a role *25*
The questions an actor must answer *45*

II On Stage 49

4 The director 51
The director's commandments *51*
Blocking *53*
Voice *58*
Script *60*

5 The designer *69*
    The three stages of design *69*
    A design model—an imaginative approach *89*
    A design model—a more realistic approach *92*

6 Behind the scenes *95*
    The stage manager *95*
    Lighting department *100*
    Sound department *101*
    Mechanists *101*
    Props *101*
    Wardrobe *102*
    Countdown to opening night *103*

7 Stage lighting *105*
    Main acting area *105*
    Specific lighting design *106*
    Lighting—a summary *112*

8 Sound *118*

III In Context *123*

9 Comedy *125*
    Origins *125*
    Comic style *128*
    Contemporary Australian comedy—a Melbourne perspective *130*

10 Drama *140*
    Origins *140*
    Contemporary movements in drama *141*
    Theatre conventions *145*

11 Theatre—the untold story *147*
    Audience—Why are we here? *147*
    Acting—the second oldest profession *155*

12 Stage versus screen *162*

13 Criticism *166*
    The search for meaning *166*
    The critic as artist *167*
    On the attack *168*
    Terminology *169*
    Deconstructing a play *170*
    The loneliness of the long distance critic *173*
    The critic as eunuch *174*

14 A dramatic interlude *178*
    Play within a play within a . . . *178*

INTRODUCTION

Where do we draw the line between classroom drama and theatre? It is not an overstatement to suggest that no two individuals would place the line in precisely the same place. There is so much overlap between drama and theatre that they are constantly drawing on each other's strengths and sharing reference points.

Drama exists without theatrical fanfare, theatre exists without the trappings of developmental drama. However individual the two, there is no debate that they are related. They are family—and family members, as we all know, should visit each other as often as possible, even if just to stay acquainted.

So much for theory. Apart from the odd homily and subjective unsubstantiated hypothesis, that is the last you will hear from me in purely theoretical terms. I am a teacher and student who likes to experience drama and theatre more than analysing or talking about them.

There is no all-encompassing correct gospel of drama and theatre—do not search for one. There are as many ways of experiencing drama and theatre as there are people on the Earth. My opinion is no more nor less valid than yours. Challenge everything I write and accept all facts and hypotheses as a stimulus to further discovery.

These most immediate of arts, drama and theatre, beg for immediacy of approach and consideration. They exist this moment and are gone the next. We may talk about them, write essays on them, film them, reflect on them and develop theories about them. Primarily, we experience them.

I have never been fond of football replays, delayed 'live' coverage or the in-depth analysis of today's news. Drama and theatre are immediate; drama is for doing and theatre is for being there.

No single text may offer you everything that you require. My choice was simple. Firstly, I could attempt to give an overview of the entire gamut of theatre and drama history and practice, allowing only cursory excursions into detail. This would offer a complete view in one sense only, historically. It would be quietly boring and perhaps unreadable.

Secondly, I could attempt, as I have done, to dive deeply into the waters. I feel safe whilst paddling in the shallows of more unknown shores. The examples chosen and the detail offered are mere guidelines to the pools that abound, should you care for a dip yourself. As you watch me splashing about, I could ask for no more than you feel inspired to join me.

The theatrical waters provide a rich treasure for those interested enough to search. In this text, I provide the map; you decide where X marks the spot and exactly which path you wish to follow to your treasure. If you decide that you need the whole map, or require more detailed directions, there is a plethora of historical and theoretical material for you to draw from. I choose not to repeat them.

The niche I have sought to address rests in the heart of drama and theatre—to learn to appreciate through the purest of all learning media—experience.

I
IN ROLE

1
A NOTE TO TEACHERS

A workshop is a way of learning. Workshops are based on the concept that that we learn better when we do rather than merely watch or listen. The learning that takes place during workshops need not be specific. In fact, the best workshops are based on discovery and exploration rather than predictable outcomes and conclusions. A workshop should be structured with firm disciplines while allowing for elements of fun, discovery, sharing and participation.

It may be a more economical use of time to learn facts, patent truths and specific value judgments from a blackboard. To spend time blindly searching for a body of knowledge known only to the leader is not generally the purpose of workshops.

WORKSHOPPING

INTRODUCTION

Do not spend too much time describing what is going to happen in the workshop or what you specifically hope to achieve. Avoid initially introducing too many related topics or possibilities. Let the participants know what the limitations of the workshop will be.

STIMULUS

A book, film, photograph or piece of music may prove more stimulating than discussion. Ensure that you choose the most suitable stimulus for your topic. Stimuli should create enough excitement and interest to generate genuine involvement and interest in the work that is to follow.

SUBJECT MATTER

Topics should be complex enough to warrant study and to have the potential to lead to areas of further learning. There should generally be potential for conflict or disagreement; providing the opportunity for the taking of a number of views (how you see things), standpoints (where you stand on the matter) and perspectives (the angle from which you are viewing).

DIRECTIONS

Ensure that instructions are precise and clearly understood by all participants. Weak and woolly directions will generate undesirable debate and questioning, leading to lack of direction in the workshop itself.

FOCUS

A workshop is run to explore complexity and subtlety rather than teach facts or truisms. True learning is discovered and experienced rather than told. This is the nature and purpose of workshops. However specific your aims and objectives, participants must be allowed to draw their own conclusions based on their workshop experiences.

GROUPING

Make use of a variety of sized groups. Each activity will have an optimum size. Different sized groups will lead to different methods of exploration and different outcomes. Ensure that each group contains a variety of types of individuals. Monitor and mix sexes, leaders, followers, levels of creativity, energy and skill, knowledge, attitude and experience.

REFLECTION

It should be standard procedure for there to be a period of consideration of the workshop experiences. Reflective periods are designed to focus and make sense of collective and individual thoughts and experiences. Periods of relection give an opportunity to synthesise and probe the experiences. This is where feelings and experiences are given sense and meaning, and turned into ideas. There are as many possible types of reflection as there are workshops.

TIMING

It is important to know when and how to respond to the ebb and flow of energy and interest. Knowing when to extend and when to complete is crucial to the process of learning and enjoyment. Introductions, stimulus, directions, participation and reflection each have an optimum time limit for a particular workshop. The group should be carefully monitored to determine flagging interest, lack of involvement and the need for more time.

QUESTIONS

Devise your workshop using these questions as a basis:

1 What, specifically, do I want participants to learn about or explore?
2 Which specific activities and structure offer the best scope for enjoyment, involvement and discovery?
3 Is there a suitable stimulus to generate interest and excitement?
4 What should I say in the introduction and how should I offer directions?
5 How should the time of the session be organised? What are my contingencies if timing does not go as planned? (Undertime—more activities or discussion; overtime—making sense of an incomplete workshop or continuing next time?)
6 Should the group be split—how and when?
7 How much guidance will I offer and how much will I allow for discovery?
8 What method(s) of reflection will I use and how much time will I allow?
9 What do I hope to achieve from the workshop?
10 What further learning or follow-up is possible?
11 Where does the workshop lie in the general scheme of things? In what context do the experiences and the workshop lie?

PHYSICALISATION

Drama brings invisible concepts and emotions into the physical world. A play, sculpture, painting or piece of music or poetry is a physical representation brought from the world of emotion and ideas. By bringing the imaginary world into the physical we are better able to consider and come to terms with complex and confronting concepts.

Playwrights write plays rather than dissertations or papers because they consider plays their most effective and evocative method of communication—their art. Teachers of drama and theatre should consider workshopping as their art—an effective and evocative method of communication and learning. The process of workshopping is one of 'physicalising' nebulous concepts.

The following are methods of 'physicalising' some complex and difficult concepts.

SOCIOGRAPHS

This term is used here not as a formal technical or medical term; merely as an invented method of description. A 'sociograph' is the physicalisation of group feelings and thoughts. It may be structured in any number of ways—just as a graph may take many forms. When meeting a group for the first time, it is vital to quickly establish a rapport with the group; to understand some of their thoughts and feelings—the misgivings, sense of anticipation and underlying fears that form the substrata of initial workshops.

(a) Ask each participant to place a hand on the right shoulder of the person they know best in the group. When this is completed, the teacher will be shown, in graphic representation, the make-up of the group. There will be singles, pairs and larger interrelated groups. Some shoulders will be empty; others full. Because the answers rely on 'knowing' rather than 'liking', the graph should not be confused with some kind of popularity contest. If the group respond sensitively, the teacher and the group will be offered a unique and graphic insight into the group's potential for working comfortably with each other.

No startling inferences may be drawn, but some trends may be apparent.

(b) Try the same exercise touching the person they know the least. One shoulder may hold many hands—indicating anything from a late starter to a solitary individual. Another may be untouched. No firm conclusions are possible, but the patterns should provide an interesting and clear representation of group thoughts and feelings.

(c) A linear graph may be created by asking participants to stand on a line which suggests some level of approval or appreciation. One end of the line will represent ten on the scale and the other nought. Participants may line up on such issues as:

- how much they are looking forward to the workshop
- how much they enjoy workshops generally
- how much they want to learn as compared to enjoy
- how experienced, comfortable or knowledgeable they feel.

Any issue on which the teacher requires an opinion may be dealt with in this way. The graph, if completed with care and sensitivity, offers a clear representation of group opinion.

Groups may congregate in the middle or polarise. One individual may line up on the opposite end of the scale to the rest of the group.

A NOTE TO TEACHERS

Place your hand on the shoulder of the person you know least. A pair, a trio and a possible problem to be addressed.

The graph is as much an indication to the group members themselves of how their opinion relates to the rest of the group as it is an indication for the teacher.

Offering opinion is too often the realm of the loudest, most lucid, most intelligent or most boisterous. A sociograph allows each group member an equality of response.

WORKING TOGETHER

(a) Groups of five start, move, complete an action and stop as if one. There must be no visible leading. When they have accomplished this, the group add their own unspoken complications.

Send two lines towards each other. When exactly will each line stop? Add a context:

- A crowd watches an airshow.
- A circus audience.

Remember, there must be no discernible leader and followers.

(b) Groups of five are equipped with pieces of dowel between 0.5 and 2 cm in diameter and between 1 and 3 metres in length. The group stand in a circle. The points of the sticks are put together, the other end is held by a group member. Whatever movement occurs, the

This is a useful exercise for working together.

points must stay together. The group must move as one, with no obvious leading.

Stance, styles of movement and position must evolve from the group. At first, only the points may move. Eventually, the circle should break and move in response to the movement of the sticks. Once the structure is firmly established, the points may be divided. Eventually even the sticks may be left. Whatever happens must be accepted by each group member.

(c) Groups of five spontaneously tell a story as one person. It will assist them to stand closely together. The group, not a single person, determines the opening, content and exact moment of conclusion.

(d) Pairs. There are moments in our lives when we feel two emotions at the same time. For instance, when chastising a child. Using abstract sound, words, movement and realistic action, the pair represent contrasting emotions—each becoming one emotion. One stands in front and one behind, and they should relate to each other. No one gives a signal to start or stop.

When the entire group is comfortable with this format, place half a dozen pairs in one line. When offered their contrasting emotions (by the rest of the group), they have one minute to discuss.

The first pair may start any time after all pairs assume a neutral position. Each pair assumes a neutral position to conclude. One pair follows another; no one should lead or offer signals.

REFLECTION

The value of reflection in the dramatic process cannot be overstated. The nature of drama and theatre tends towards the experiential and the immediate. In such circumstances, the broader context of learning may be lost in the heat of personal involvement and response.

It is vital that all sessions conclude with a period of reflection that assists participants to assess their experiences and to view them in a broader context.

A FORMAT EXAMPLE

The circle response

At the conclusion of a rehearsal or workshop, everyone is seated in a circle. The person on the leader's left generally starts. Each participant offers an honest and personal appraisal or response to any aspect of the rehearsal or workshop. They should strive for a detailed and personal response, not just whether they liked or disliked something. Participants should be sensitive to the nature of personal comment and the amount of time that they take up. Participants may comment on previous responses. There are two rules—no participant may be challenged or interrupted while speaking and everyone must wait their turn.

Those without anything to say may simply pass. The leader is generally last. This is where summing up, drawing together and further responses may be allowed.

Generally, a strong mood of reflection will be created which will be indicative of the standard and depth of rehearsal or workshop which has just taken place. The circle response is an excellent gauge of the success of a workshop. Each participant is guaranteed a considered and reflective audience for their views and, therefore, these views tend to be considered and personal. Everyone has an equal opportunity to respond in their own time.

THE BOOK

Any individual workshop or rehearsal will generally be one in a series leading towards a set goal—be it a performance or the completion of a course. Although it is important for each individual to record the experiences and responses, the bulk of work completed during workshops and rehearsals is group work. This suggests that a group, as well as a personal response, is required.

The nature of private journals is such that they may not be shared or collated. A shared book allows public expression of personal opinions and ideas.

The book may contain:

- the accumulation of script ideas and dialogue as they occur in each session
- an accurate record of what takes place in each session
- ideas and personal responses from any group members
- an accurate record of the circle response or any other reflective sessions.

The book may be hard-backed or a collection of A4 pages. One group member should take responsibility for the book each session. It is this person's role to ensure that the book is completed accurately and in detail. This may require this individual to play a lesser role in the activities which take place during the session.

Group members should be encouraged to read and to contribute to the book as often as possible, as well as completing their own individual workbooks.

The book may be regularly photocopied so that every individual has greater access. Alternatively, photocopies at the conclusion of a course, rehearsal or process may provide an excellent record for participants.

JOURNALS OR WORKBOOKS

By nature and definition, journals tend to be personal and sometimes private documents. It is important to determine early who the audience for a journal will be. Is it a private monologue? Will it be addressed from the writer to the teacher/director? Will the teacher/director answer and turn it into a dialogue? Will other members of the group be given access?

If an adequate shared record is kept in the book, this then frees individual journals from recording every circumstance of a session and allows greater scope for personal responses and format. The shared volume will contain details of specific activities. Journals should contain details of exactly how individuals were affected or influenced by these activities; whether they enjoyed the session or learned anything of value. The journal provides an opportunity for detailed personal analysis of every aspect of a workshop or rehearsal session.

QUESTIONS

Students should consider these questions after each workshop:

1 What specifically did we do?
2 How was the session structured?
3 What were the immediate goals of the person leading the session?
4 How do these relate to our long-term goals?
5 Can I see a clear direction in what we are doing?
6 Were the activities well chosen for their required purpose?
7 Was the session timed and structured well?
8 What overall impression was I left with?
9 Was the session predictable or open to discovery?
10 Were directions clearly given?
11 Was there an adequate reflective period?
12 How much enjoyment or satisfaction did I gain?
13 How challenging were the activities?
14 How much did I learn?
15 How important was the session?
16 How does this session relate to others we have done?

2
FROM WORKSHOP TO STAGE

For many, the jump from workshop to stage seems an uncrossable chasm. This need not be the case. Workshops are not isolated from performance; they are an integral part of building a performance. Aspects of workshops covered in this chapter are:

Characters (the who)
Themes (the what)
Structure (the how)
Scenes and settings (the where)
Time (the when)
Motivation (the why)
Development (the what-then)
Some approaches to script

CHARACTERS (THE WHO)

EMPATHY

The success of all plays depends on the quality of the characters who inhabit them. A play is a vicarious experience and each audience member must feel empathy with the characters. The protagonist(s), the hero, generally undertakes a dramatic journey, with conflict provided by the antagonist(s). The protagonist(s) provides the point of view from which the audience views the twists and turns of the plot.

2D OR NOT 2D?

That is the question. Stereotypes are character types who we know well enough to complete the details of a character from minimal evidence. The danger with this type of character is that the more a character becomes a type the less real the character may appear.

DETAILS

We learn primarily about characters by what they do and say. Hearing about one character from another is not generally the best method of expounding character detail.

A play is a slice of time taken from the lives of particular individuals. Carefully chosen, a slice of time may prove to be the most important moment from a person's entire lifetime.

We cannot know everything about a character. Each character detail should be carefully chosen and added as a piece of jigsaw to the audience's total understanding of the character as a human being.

Great depth may be created and suggested from the simplest and most minimal of details. The best playwrights are experts in providing shorthand details which provide enough outline for the audience to add their own colours and depth.

PAST AND FUTURE

All characters are coming from and going to something. No matter how real the time on stage, there must be the suggestion of a greater time frame.

DEVELOPMENT

It is generally accepted that in plays at least one of the characters will learn or have a change of heart or opinion as a direct result of the encounters experienced in the play. The best plays tend to revolve around people rather than a plot, character rather than circumstance.

ACTIVITIES

1 Getting into role

All members of the group sit on chairs in a circle. For fun, any number of versions of musical chairs could be played to determine who sits in 'the hot seat'. This is, however, peripheral to the focus of the activity.

The individual in possession of the hot seat is, in role, required to answer questions put by the rest of the group. Initially, this person may have very little idea of the character who they will become. With each succeeding question and answer, more details are added to the total picture of the character. As voice, mannerism and gesture become appropriate, these may be added to the character.

The initial questions such as, 'what is your name?', 'where do you live?' and 'what do you do?' should be followed by more probing questions whose answers will provide increasing insight into the individual.

Once the character is clearly and credibly established, the person leaves the hot seat and rejoins the circle. All further questioning from this character to other possessors of the hot seat will be in role.

Eventually an entire circle of questioners will be in role, with each successive question and answer adding still greater detail to the character of both questioner and respondent.

With everyone in role, add these circumstances:

(a) Participants are residents of a block of flats which is to be bulldozed. The owner answers questions from the group and then leaves. Residents decide their next step.

(b) Participants are present at a school council meeting which has been called to consider allegations made by one of their number. The principal convenes the meeting.

2 Character types

Form groups of five. Improvising in a given situation, each group member takes on a distinct character type. The improvisation is interrupted periodically to revolve the character types. The improvisation is complete when all group members have been all types. The actual characters remain the same throughout and a consistency of plotline must be maintained. It is only the types that change. Try the following improvisations:

The meeting
1 wants to leave early
2 wants to explore more deeply
3 wants to mediate
4 wants to lead
5 wants to go along.
or
1 agrees with everyone
2 disagrees with everyone
3 likes to organise

4 is in a hurry
5 strays from the point.

Peers
1 wants to be liked
2 is the natural leader
3 is lacking confidence
4 is afraid of wrong-doing
5 is excited by danger or wrong-doing.

Dinner party
1 is interested in others
2 is interested in self
3 maintains a single train of thought
4 has scattered thoughts
5 likes to steer the conversation.

Invent your own situation and character types.

THEMES (THE WHAT)

SUBJECT

The participants should have some affinity with and care about whatever theme or topic is chosen.

RESEARCH

Research can unearth specific concepts and ideas which lend themselves to theatre. Research will also create involvement and give added significance and detail to little-known topics.

DISCUSSION

Discussion is important but should not be allowed to totally dominate. Workshops are excellent methods of exploring possible topics and generating new ideas. Scriptwriting and ideas sessions can and should be just as much active, discovery periods as any other session of drama.

PLOT AND SUBPLOT

The plot of many of the best plays may be summed up in a single sentence. That is not to say that they lack action but that the storyline is centred around one basic situation.

Intertwined with this one major happening, a series of minor happenings, or subplots will generally be weaved. Whereas a particular play may be about A (the plot), a particular scene may be about B or C (subplots), with B and C contributing in some way to our understanding of A.

If it is impossible to economically sum up what a play is 'about' this may suggest a lack of focus on the part of the playwright. A play which purports to be about everything or anything may find itself to be about very little indeed.

NARRATIVE

Whatever your approach, your role is to unfold a kind of story or experience for your audience. Your audience must care about your developing plot and be interested enough to wait for the outcome.

ACTIVITIES

1 (a) Bring to class something which has a particular meaning or significance for you, such as a film, photograph, drawing, piece of music or piece of jewellery.

  (b) Describe what the item means to you or, preferably, show the item's significance through a piece of drama. This need not have words and may involve individuals and groups.

2 (a) Bring to class an interesting or significant family photograph. It may be aged or recent. A photocopy will do if it is brittle or precious. If this is difficult, an anonymous newspaper or magazine photograph will suffice. Where possible, group members, by interviewing a member of their own family, will find out as much about the photograph as possible. Fictitious stories may be invented for the newspaper and magazine photographs. Everyone will also bring their own photograph.

   Photographs will be laid out (and mounted, if possible without damage) on a large board as if all the photographs were part of the same family history. Each photograph will be accompanied by a paragraph of information.

   Where little or no information is available about a photograph, this will be invented by the group. The most recent members of the family, at this stage, will be photographs of the group members.

   Next, making use of pictures from books, newspapers and magazines, the family tree will be taken into the future at least another two generations.

> (b) In groups of five and using family members as characters, perform a piece based on any period in this family's history, including the future. What has happened to this family to make their history significant?

STRUCTURE (THE HOW)

EXPRESSION

Theatrically, there are better and worse ways of expressing yourself. The most appropriate method of expression should be chosen for the performance as a whole and individual scenes.

STAGING

Consider staging, lighting and effects. Does the group want to work on stage in theatre; with sets and costumes; with audience in front or around; with music, band or orchestra; with lighting and special effects? What combinations of music, drama and dance will be incorporated?

STYLE

We tend to regard the proscenium arch as the 'traditional' style of presentation. Although considered to be 'natural', it may claim no more natural role than, say, a Greek amphitheatre or theatre-in-the-round.

Theatre is not an exact slice of life. Theatre is a piece of life prodded and poked, moulded and manipulated, extended and exaggerated. Theatre was never meant to be life—it is meant to pass comment on life. As such, in theatre, reality is never what it seems. As Aristotle said, 'A play is an imitation of action, and not the action itself.'

Style is about statement, not reality. There are better and worse ways to make your point. Realism is merely one of your choices.

Acting style may range from realistic to stylised or abstract. Your content may be realistic, exaggerated, absurd or symbolic. Your style should reflect your purpose. You must decide whether you wish to teach, entertain or provoke.

ACTIVITY

Work in groups of four. Each member of the group brings a drawing, photograph, song, script or story from a newspaper—anything that lends itself to presentation. The group considers each item and chooses one for presentation. Groups will offer two presentations based on contrasting styles. If you require assistance in choosing a style, mix and match columns A, B and C.

A	B	C
Drama	Abstract	Story-based
Comedy	Realistic	Emotion-based
Musical	Exaggerated	Skill-based
Dance		Theme-based
Melodrama		Design-based
		Impro-based
		Script-based

SCENES AND SETTINGS (THE WHERE)

Public and private areas offer extreme contrasts of mood. A park allows many different characters, unknown to each other, to enter and leave; a room allows opportunity for paranoia, siege or security.

Playwrights need to consider the practical implications of scene changes. Numerous changes may disrupt the flow of action; fewer may lead to boredom or a stifled plot-line. By way of imagination, scenes may be changed or adapted at will. If complicated three-dimensional realistic sets are required, it is preferable to have fewer scene changes.

ACTIVITY

Work in groups of five. The object of the activity is to perform two scenes which have the same basic content, but which are entirely different because of their respective settings. Imagine, for instance, an intimate romantic supper first in a restaurant and then on a roof or in a park. The characters and meal will be the same, but the circumstances will vary because of the nature of the settings.

TIME (THE WHEN)

The concept of time refers not only to a particular moment on stage, but also the total time frame of a piece. A play may last three hours, but seldom does a play cover only three consecutive hours from the lives of the characters. Three hours is enough to include an entire lifetime—a sobering thought.

ACTIVITY

Work in groups of five. Each group chooses a famous or interesting character. The character may be real, from fiction or invented by the group. The object of the exercise is to present an insight into the character through two scenes which are linked by time.

If you require assistance, here are some related time frames:

(a) The moments of birth and death.
(b) Scenes decades or years apart.
(c) Two different times on the same day.
(d) Two different meals.
(e) Two related incidents.
(f) Two moments of tragedy or great excitement.
(g) A night and the following morning.
(h) The same time on two consecutive days.
(i) Two Christmases.

MOTIVATION (THE WHY)

This not only refers to the characters, but also to the twists in the plot. Explaining why and how things occur is one of the basic skills of playwriting. Knowing that one person shoots another is not enough. The playwright needs to provide insight into why the shooting took place and what circumstances led up to the shooting.

Playwrights determine their own rules of reality and this allows great freedom in determining why events occur or characters act as they do. Why does a clown walk into a cupboard instead of out of the door? If the reality that the playwright has created is topsy-turvey, full of the unusual and unexpected, the clown's action will seem to be entirely logical.

It is the responsibility of the playwright to maintain this reality once it is established. A playwright is allowed to include surprising, illogical or unexpected twists, but inconsistencies must be approached with great care. Plots with logical substance are most able to accept a twist. Loose, nebulous plots tend to disappear into a puff of nothingness at the slightest inconsistency.

Audiences are not generally accepting of lurches from one reality or set of rules to another. It is difficult enough to enter the world of the playwright, without the playwright jumping from one reality to another. If the clown leaves the cupboard and starts shooting people with a machine-gun, an entirely new reality has been established. The 'why', the motivation for all actors and action, becomes changed.

A number of plays and films have used changes in perceptions of reality as the core of their action. In Tom Stoppard's, *The Real Inspector Hound*, for instance, he has a real audience facing a staged audience. The reality of a murder mystery takes on added dimensions when an audience member enters the set. When this audience member becomes the next victim, the stakes are increased considerably. A number of films have dealt with the concept of actors leaving the screen to join the viewing audience.

ACTIVITY

Form groups of any size. Put simply, groups must surprise the audience. A piece is to be established and then to take such an unexpected turn that it will catch the audience unprepared. If you can imagine two reels from quite different films spliced together, this will give you some idea of how to approach this task.

For example:

Shirley Temple meets the Wolf Man

Indiana Jones and the Temple of Disneyland

Friday the 13th—Part IV—ET returns

Jaws III—The Empire Strikes Back.

Your difficulty will be to ensure that your characters are able to jump the reality gap which you establish.

Scenes from a Shakespearean tragedy and comedy would be equally incongruous as the above films, as would the writings of say, two playwrights such as Tom Stoppard and Harold Pinter.

DEVELOPMENT (THE WHAT-THEN)

A virtual unbroken rule of playwriting—and you will have realised by now that there are very few of these—is that something has to happen. A play is often regarded as a type of theatrical journey undertaken by the protagonist(s). At the conclusion of the journey something will have happened to change the protagonist(s) or to change our (the audience's) perception of the protagonist(s).

Ideally, the audience should feel that they have participated in this journey, learned something about the characters and even, perhaps, themselves.

The developments in a plot need to be gradually unfolded and carefully timed. A playwright produces an individual deck and holds each card close to the chest, waiting for the exact moment to play the trump card—the moment of maximum impact. The greatest story ever told may be made to sound mediocre if not unfolded correctly.

ACTIVITY

Divide your favourite story (even a nursery rhyme, such as 'Jack and the Beanstalk', will do) into at least four scenes. Each scene will be used to unfold at least one aspect of character and one twist in the plot. Initially, lay the scenes out in chronological order. Write each of the scenes on a separate piece of paper. Now experiment with the order of these scenes. Try to find a logical progression other than chronological. How do the alternatives compare to chronological development?

SOME APPROACHES TO SCRIPT

Historical and traditional based

Greek tragedy, mystery/miracle plays, cycles, fairground, wandering players, music hall, circus, vaudeville, cabaret, theatre restaurant; period conventions; research required.

Improvisation based

Workshopping, energy, group-based, actor as centre-piece; strong structure for improvisation required.

Story based

Adaptations of folk tales, nursery rhymes, children's stories, poems, myths, legends, epic tales; exploring methods of storytelling.

Music based

Music/drama, folk music dramatised, rock musicals, musicals; use of music as an expressive form; some musical skills required.

Process based

Where the presentation makes visible the production and development process; show within a show; minimising theatrical effect for truth.

Skills based

Mime, dance; formal disciplined expressions; pure skill or talent; juggling, tumbling, magic, puppetry.

Art based

Pure artistic expression; blurring the boundaries between art forms.

Script based

Theatre from the written word; original or derived; piece or collection; whole or extract; individual or group-devised.

Theme based

Umbrella construction over one central concept or idea.

Design based

Visual presentation using actors for much more than aural qualities; visual and design considerations override the constraints of plot and character.

ACTIVITY

Across the top of a page write these headings:

WHO   WHAT   HOW   WHERE   WHEN   WHY   WHAT-THEN

Divide into groups of five. Each group is to present a scene which mixes and matches details from each heading. Groups should develop their plots so that 'what' logically leads onto 'what then'. This might not be as easy as it sounds as both may bear little relation to each other.

The following are general categories from which you may choose your specific examples:

WHO	WHAT	HOW	WHERE	WHEN	WHY	WHAT-THEN
occupations	intrigue	monologue	public	before	insanity	resolution
mannerisms	crime	dialogue	private	after	luck	development
physical traits	relationships	improvised	internal	during	coincidence	achievement
habits	morals	scripted	external	time of day	fate	failure
gestures	society	lyrical	work	year	will	learning
age	people	colloquial	play	season	obligation	completion
personality	domestic	fragmented	real	meal	religion	new beginning
famous	argument	realistic	imagined	celebration	duty	arrival
fictional	agreement	abstract	fantasy	period	love	discovery
heroes	enquiry	stylised	country	historical	fear	reward
villains	request	absurd	city	contemporary	hunger	revenge
sporting	challenge	comic	planet	future	jealousy	come-uppance
nationality	conflict	tragic	a space	birthday	hatred	growth

3
CREATING A ROLE

The script upon which characters are based provides only the bones, the outline for an actor. Flesh must be provided by the director/teacher in tandem with the actor. Ultimately, the actor stands alone. On stage, once the character has developed to a certain level, the director's contribution becomes minimal and relates mainly to external details such as where or how a character should stand. It then becomes the actor's almost sole responsibility to add ever-increasing detail and depth to the character being portrayed.

In class, a teacher tends to establish situations where characters may develop. The characters, however, tend to be the product of each individual's imagination. It is vital for strategies to be developed to assist the creation and taking on of role. The ten steps listed are not to be followed in order and may be freely drawn upon. They provide a framework—stimulus points—upon which a role may be hung. Not all steps will apply to all roles.

THE VALUE OF ROLE-PLAY

This text does not advocate the use of one style of drama or context over another, but strongly suggests a variety of experiences and approaches.

We may use role to learn virtually anything. Specifically, from role we may learn:

- to stand in the shoes of another
- appropriate responses

- to feel
- to develop awareness
- to have fun
- to appreciate the seriousness or complexity of situations
- to consider repercussions and implications
- to be free of personal constraints
- decision-making
- and more.

All this from simple practical activities based on role play. The most basic activities may provide the springboard for the most profound learning. It is vital to note that profound learning is more likely to be derived from excellent teaching than excellent textbooks.

Little space has been given over to the mechanisms of reflection or the methods and techniques of placing practical work into a broader context. That has been left to the teacher/leader. The content of a course of learning may be derived from text(s); the context must be determined by the teacher/leader.

METHODS OF CREATING A ROLE

In this section we will examine methods of creating a role. Each method is followed by activities. The methods are:

Motivation/thoughts
Research
Observation
Reaction
Script
Physicality
Before and After
Voice
Inner Pulse
Self

MOTIVATION/THOUGHTS

A director/teacher can tell you what to do but only you know what you are thinking as you follow directions. To come to life, a character must respond as a human being—not an unfeeling automaton. At any given moment there may be thousands of thoughts filtering through the brain. In the normal scheme of things we choose a few of these thoughts to govern our actions:

- I am hungry
- I will eat that piece of cake
- But it isn't good for me
- I love chocolate so much
- It is the last piece

And so it continues until it finally resolves itself with action. It is not enough for an actor to walk over to a piece of cake and eat it because the director said 'eat'. In real life there is no director—we must make our own decisions—and so it must seem on the stage.

ACTIVITIES

1 Choose a simple action, one that may be completed without undue difficulty or complication.
    (a) Complete the action in as neutral a manner as possible.
    (b) Next, add a reason to complete the action—through your manner and intention make your reason very clear. Try at least five of these.
    (c) Choose two conflicting thoughts which govern the action (should I?/shouldn't I?).
    (d) The hard part: How much depth can you create for your character? How many conflicting and complementary thoughts/intentions/motivations can you provide for your action? How clearly can you portray this to an audience?
2 Follow the same process but this time include a line of dialogue.
3 Understanding why a character acts in a particular way is called *motivation*. Actors need to understand why a character says or does the things that are asked for in the script. Although an audience may still fear or dislike an evil character, if they understand why an evil character acts in a particular way, they will be more involved.
    (a) Look at some picture books and films that have 'baddies'. Which of the 'baddies' have a reason to be bad and which are simply bad?
    (b) Do you know of any 'baddies' who are actually likeable?
    (c) Boris Karloff was the first actor to play Frankenstein's monster as if he had a heart. Which monsters do you know who have hearts and which are just plain monsters?

CREATING A ROLE 27

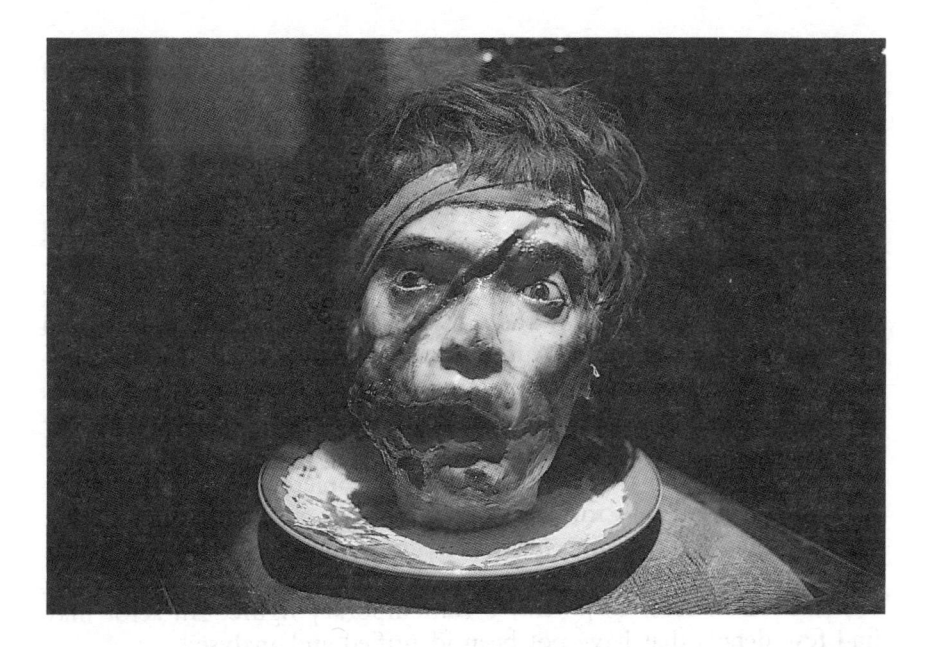

A head has feelings too. Assuming it has life, what could possibly motivate this head?
(Photo courtesy the Victorian Arts Centre, from a Performing Arts Museum display.)

(d) How would you act these characters to show the audience that although evil, you still have feelings?

- the big bad wolf from Little Red Riding Hood
- Dracula
- a witch
- a gangster
- a punk who robs old ladies
- Prince John (from Robin Hood)
- the Wicked Queen from Snow White
- a corrupt police officer or politician
- the president who pushes the button
- a soldier responsible for a massacre
- a thief or shoplifter.

Put them in a play and see what happens.

RESEARCH

An actor should find out as much as possible about the character to be played. All details, no matter how small, may help the actor to flesh out the character as a person. After all, imagine the number of incidents that have come together to create you as the person you are now. You may be afraid of dogs because of something that occurred when you were two years old; you may eat quickly because you come from a big family; you may do bad things because other people have always treated you badly.

Historical and famous characters generally require research to discover relevant aspects of personality. Unfortunately, many of the pertinent details required by the actor are not to be found in historical documents or biographies. Autobiographies may tell us what the subject thought but not what impression this had on others. Biographies may cover the effect the character had on others but very few of the details of what made the character tick.

Future generations of actors will have a plethora of details from which to derive details for characterisation. No public figure in the last fifty years has escaped the most searching scrutiny. In fact, we seem to understand our public figures with such intimacy that it is extremely difficult for an actor to portray a contemporary figure. An actor may find few details that have not been identified and analysed.

Not so historical figures from the past—pre-media we may call them. A rumour seems to have spread that Napoleon spent a lot of time with one hand in his jacket but surely characterisation requires much more than this. We know he won many battles and lost the Battle of Waterloo. This is general knowledge but an actor needs more. An actor must know 'why'.

- Why did Napoleon choose to wage war?
- Why did others follow him?
- Why did he have himself crowned emperor?
- Tactics aside, why was he finally beaten?

In the example of Napoleon, the material may be there for the gleaning. Details of Lady Hamilton and Josephine may not be so forthcoming. Acting a famous female character poses the added difficulty that historical documents are traditionally masculine in orientation.

What of lesser characters — the not-so-famous — Everyman and Everywoman—the so-called normals who will seldom make the front page of the tabloids or the first verse of a troubadour's ballad? How do we find out about them?

In fact, some of our most accurate history is based on the everyday lives of mere mortals. Their stories are tales untarnished by the exaggerations of storytellers and balladeers. After the ancient publicity machines took over the story of Napoleon, how could we ever hope to glean the real person from the image? Will we ever truly understand characters so much larger than life that they would barely rest easily in the pages of even a comic strip?

An actor must learn to decipher and edit. A portrayal cannot consist of every single detail pertaining to a particular character. An actor must develop an eye for the vital and the basic, and learn which details are merely fat—to be stored and only used if absolutely necessary.

ACTIVITIES

1 From any media source, choose a contemporary character who is of interest to you. Avoid a famous character.
   (a) Lacking details of the individual, discover as much information as you are able regarding the person's likely situation, e.g.:
   - where they live
   - socio-economic status
   - likely aspirations and fears
   - likely family structure
   - likely cares and woes.

   Notice that we are entering the areas of the detective and just plain guesswork.

   (b) From your, hopefully, copious amount of information and summation, determine which details you regard as relevant to characterisation.
   (c) Attempt to bring the character to life. Search for:
   - key phrase(s)
   - a method of walking/stance
   - voice inflection(s)
   - gesture
   - habit(s) (repetitive behaviour)
   - likely situation.

   (d) Write a short monologue to allow you to explore the character in detail.

2 Take your character back to a period in history of your own choosing. It should be as if the same person has been born into a different time. The experiences and pressures will have been entirely different. The learning and developmental processes will have been different and may have created an almost totally different personality. Once again avoid famous characters.
   (a) Follow the same processes that you used to create your first character.

(b) Write a monologue which makes clear that we are viewing one person in two distinct situations rather than two completely different characters.

(c) Find out as much as you can about your favourite character from history. Find out about eating, sleeping, home, friends, family, occupation, habits—anything that will assist you to understand this person and create a role for them. See if you can find out why they did certain things. You know that Napoleon started wars—do you know why? Decide what is interesting and what is irrelevant.

3 Use some of what you have learned (research material) to act as this person. Write a speech for your character and 'deliver' it as if you were that person. Put three or four of these characters into a play:

(a) at a bus stop

(b) at a parent–teacher night

(c) on a battlefield

(d) on a train

(e) at a football match

(f) in a castle

(g) in the outback.

OBSERVATION

Actors use everyone around them and everything that happens to them as the raw material to develop characters. Actors have to constantly be aware of the details of real situations and consider how to adapt real life to the stage. Real life is long and not very interesting to watch—meals take thirty minutes, buying a carton of milk may take longer. Actors need to take the essence of these experiences and shorten them to heighten their interest. Actors create roles by combining the characteristics of many, possibly boring people together to make one interesting person.

Most of us will walk through a crowded street searching for gaps between people and wishing that they would get out of the way. An actor, on the other hand, is not particularly interested in the gaps. An actor may want to know why a certain person is looking so glum, or why someone is in such a hurry. An actor may look closely at the way a woman holds her handbag or how a man parts his hair, even what two people do with their hands as they are arguing. One stage character may be composed of details from hundreds of people, incidents and situations.

CREATING A ROLE

What specific character details are evident?

ACTIVITIES

1 Have everyone in your class invent a character. The descriptions should be very simple, like 'old crabby lady', 'nice postman', 'smart alec', 'painful little brother'. All of the characters should be written on small separate pieces of paper. Everyone then chooses a character out of a hat.

When you have your character your next job is to find out as much as you possibly can about this person:

- What is their name?
- What do they eat?
- Where do they live?
- What makes them happy or angry?
- Why do they do things?

When you have worked out some general ideas, find more details from real people and events. For the next two days find people like your character. In particular, keep your eyes open in public places such as trains, streets, sports fields, shops or schoolyards. How do they walk, talk, wave their arms, eat? What newspaper do they prefer? What do they carry? What clothes do they wear?

Write down every detail that you think could have even the slightest interest or relevance to your character. Decide which details you believe are important and which you would rather leave out.

When everyone in the class has some ideas about their character try placing them in some situations such as:

- old schoolfriends meeting after many years
- a shopkeeper who short changes all of his customers
- at a football match that is very close
- a crime on a crowded street
- vandalism on a crowded train
- in an enchanted wood
- in the court of Camelot.

The best actors have an excellent eye for detail. This does not mean that they stare at everyone and everything and note every detail that occurs. Observing is a matter of determining which incidents and characteristics could contribute to the formation of a character. We are the product of many thousands of experiences and events and our complex natures are a reflection of these experiences. At any given moment we may be displaying any one of our thousand faces or masks. Actors seldom 'recreate' people that they have observed. They choose pertinent details from perhaps hundreds of people and amalgamate them into a distinct personality.

2 Next time you are in a public place, observe. Choose one individual and try to learn as much as possible about this individual. How do they react to particular situations? Choose another character—and another. Look for physical details as well as details of personality. Note only those details which could be of use to you in creating a role.

   (a) Add to your monologue delivery specific details which you have acquired through observation—choose either your contemporary or historical monologue.

   (b) Create a character of your own choosing which has at least ten details which you have observed. Try not to 'invent' details. Depend almost solely on characteristics you have derived from 'real' life.

REACTION

The characters invented by actors would be highly unreal if they were simply an assorted set of observations. 'Acting' is not quite the right word for what happens on stage. In fact, actors spend much of their time reacting rather than acting. That is, they are placed in a situation and react as their character would. If they were to simply act, the audience would see this as false. Actors must learn to think rapidly and always be ready to adapt to the cues offered by the other characters. There is no such thing as stock anger: 'When she comes at me I will give her my usual angry look'. Anger is reaction to an ill done to the character.

General moves must be worked out beforehand (blocked) but each movement must be a logical answer to a previous movement. For instance, for a sword-fight to work on stage an actor must react to the movements of the opponent and try not to anticipate the next move.

Basing characters on animals is an excellent way of developing reaction. Animals depend on simple and clear instincts, such as fear and hunger, for their actions (motivation). The ability to act without thinking is known as *spontaneity*.

ACTIVITIES

1 Choreograph a sword fight between two characters using something harmless (like cardboard tubes) as swords. Use only six movements and have each character memorise the movements. Act out a fight in two ways:

   (a) with each actor woodenly acting out the movements

   (b) with the actors reacting to each other and each other's movements.

2 With the group in a circle, one person steps forward and says how they are feeling.

   'I am feeling . . .'

   The next person makes a sound and movement that best sums up this feeling. The whole group repeats this sound and movement. The second person then says how they are feeling, and so on. Make sure that there is sound with every movement and that the movements use the whole body and not just the head or arms. People are usually only embarrassed when they are half-hearted and hanging back. The more energy the group uses the easier it is to do.

3 Which animal qualities are possessed by your favourite character from myth or legend?

4 Choose your favourite animal and start to develop some of its characteristics.
  (a) How does it walk, talk, sleep, eat? What habits does it have?
  (b) Your animal is starving—how does it react?
  (c) A bushfire sweeps through the room.
  (d) Two hunters with guns are sighted.
  (e) Move around and start to meet some other animals, greet them with your own peculiar sound.
  (f) Imagine that you are not an animal but a person with animal characteristics—what sort of person are you? What do you do for a living? How do you walk, talk, eat, meet people?
  (g) Move around and meet some of the other people with animal characteristics.
  (h) Become more human so that the character you are playing is a person, but still retaining strong animal characteristics. Have three or four of these characters meet—
  - in a posh restaurant
  - on a roller coaster

What human characteristics are possessed by this animal?

CREATING A ROLE 35

- on a plane about to crash
- in a bank.

(i) Create the Court of Camelot with everyone becoming a knight or lady with animal qualities. Invent a name such as 'Sir Puppy the Faithful' or 'Lady Kookaburra the Talkative'. A threat comes to the Court of Camelot. What happens?

(j) A visit to the zoo to either perform or observe could provide some interesting follow-up.

SCRIPT

When all is said and done, an actor finds most ideas about the character from the script. Scripts tell you as much as the playwright believes you should know. Some playwrights give extensive stage directions and describe the characters in intricate detail. Others offer general guidelines, and leave the rest up to the imagination of the director and the actors. It is the role of the director to decide what the playwright intended. Although actors contribute ideas it is the director who has final say with regard to *interpretation* (what it all means) and *presentation* (how it will be shown). Scripts are merely words which may be delivered in a thousand different ways. The following activities deal with presentation.

ACTIVITIES

1 Which emotions do you believe are most closely associated with these colours?
   (a) brown
   (b) green
   (c) purple
   (d) red
   (e) white
   (f) black
   (g) puce
   What are your most and least favoured colours? Why?

2 Choose some lines from a script and read them as if they were a particular colour. Change colour. How does the meaning change?

3 Work in groups of four. Each group chooses one line from a script and presents two scenes which use the line in a different way.

4 Work in groups of five. There will be four actors and a director. Each group must present a production of script in a particular way. The director chooses the method of presentation:

(a) a comedy

(b) a tragedy

(c) a fairy tale

(d) a spy thriller

(e) a soap opera

(f) a TV game show.

It is the director's role to help the actors to present their piece as clearly as possible. If the words are a problem, make up your own words or memorise.

5 Read a piece of script over two contrasting pieces of music. How does the music change the mood and colour of the reading?

Any line of text may be read in a number of ways. The context of each line is most important:

- Who is making the statement?
- What is the character attempting to say?
- Why is the statement being made?
- Where does the line fit in the play?

It is assumed that each character on the stage has a history that contains a multitude of memories and experiences. Any one of these experiences may be drawn on to interpret and deliver a line.

It is an excellent technique to focus on one aspect of interpretation for each rehearsal. For instance, assume two characters, now strangers, have had a relationship in the distant past. Play the scene first focusing primarily on the past relationship. See what changes occur when the focus is moved to their families. Next, concentrate on the coldness between them. Finally, complete the scene with whatever focus seems most appropriate and applicable to a particular line of dialogue. Hopefully the final presentation will contain the greatest depth of meaning—incorporating many elements.

Proceed now to the following activities, which deal with interpretation.

ACTIVITIES

1 As an improvisation exercise, try the above scene ensuring that each point of concentration is covered. The script should remain

unaltered for each piece. Repeat the scene, inventing your own points of concentration. It may prove difficult to make these clear to the audience.

2 Try mixing some of the following activities and points of concentration:

Activity	Point of concentration
Walk the dog	You have lost your best friend
Bake a cake	You have been stood up
Comb your hair	You have won some money
Get dressed	You have just had an argument
Do homework	You are worried about your future
Weed the garden	You are waiting for something/someone important
Kick a football	Your life is a mess

3 Two people start an improvisation. Freeze the improvisation midstream and offer additional points of concentration. For instance, two people may be rowing a boat. At a given moment one character is told that the second is a murderer. This information may be offered secretly or shared. The second character may also be offered additional information. The two characters should only subtly alter the portrayal to include the new points of concentration. The main thrust of the scene should be unaltered but simply have a new aspect added. See how many additional aspects it is possible to include before the scene begins to fall apart.

PHYSICALITY

Traits

Some people have physical characteristics which completely dominate all else. Sometimes these characteristics are not the product of personality—they determine personality. A limp is physical but may colour a characterisation to such an extent that all details of portrayal seem to depend on the limp. Anger and frustration become by-products of coping with the handicap. All aspirations may be coloured by the basic aspiration to walk without difficulty.

A positive gait (step) may help to create a purposeful character rather than merely being one detail of a positive characterisation. The gait may become central to all else—the frame upon which all other characteristics are hung. Gesture may also take this central role. Certain gestures such as scratching, use of the hands and arms, pointing or hands on hips may be the crucial—the pivotal—details in the creation of character. There is a subtle difference here, but we are talking of character being created from the physical rather than the physical being regarded as merely one detail of an overall characterisation.

ACTIVITIES

1 Create a monologue allowing physicality to completely dominate the delivery. Characterisation must develop from a physical characteristic—it must dominate all else.

2 Now put the physical characteristic back into perspective. Although it exists, make a genuine attempt to hide it. Sometimes we are aware of and become self-conscious of our physical characteristics. Attempt a portrayal where a physical trait is being carefully masked from the audience by the performer. Try a scene where a number of characters attempt to hide physical characteristics from each other.

Mime

The nature of improvisation, by definition, often requires that the performer also be the writer. In some cases, emotions and free expression may be stifled by the basic inability of a performer to find just the right words for the particular circumstance.

Working from a set script is not the answer, as this may stifle much of the spontaneity that is the hallmark of great improvisation. Is there a solution?

Some characters may be brought to life without the use of words. There are many qualities unrelated to speech which a character may communicate.

The art of mime is not exclusively related to the illusion of making real something which does not exist. Illusory mime is merely one facet of acting without words. The core of the art, as in all acting, is to create a real character to whom an audience may relate.

Freeing the actor from words may offer a greater scope for characterisation. Objects and animals, without the constraints of speech may, perhaps, be more readily brought to life. Just as puppetry allows the actor to create the impossible, so mime extends the vocabulary of the actor beyond the real, the mundane, the everyday.

Mime is an art form that requires constant repetitious practice to achieve the highest standards of clarity and expression. However, remembering a few basic rules will assist even the novice mimer to achieve communication without the use of voice.

Delineation. Start and finish each movement with exactness. Snap movements to start and stop rather than glide them. Meandering movements lack clarity and shape. Always complete movements, do not let them peter out. Never create and forget—once an object is established, it exists; do not just ignore it unless you specifically want it forgotten.

Try pouring a drink from a bottle into a glass. Where are the glass and bottle? What is the drink? Where are the bottle and glass placed when no longer required?

Touch. Because touch is the mechanism of creation, there must be as much touch as possible. Think of any excuse at all to touch a surface. If the lights are out, we need to feel our way along a wall; if we are cleaning a surface we can delineate it; if we pat a dog, we can show its size; we can place our hands on one surface to reach up to another. Looking will seldom be enough to show an audience the required details. The hands and body provide the signals for the audience. When not being touched or used, an object will tend to simply cease to exist.

Try pouring the same drink. This time think of an excuse to touch as many surfaces as possible, including the path to the kitchen.

Impulse and isolation. Some objects we act upon, others create forces that act upon us. I can open a door, but it also can slam back in my face; I can pick up a dog, it can also run away from me, dragging me behind it. To display this clearly to an audience I need to show a force acting upon a particular part of my body—with the rest of the body compensating for and adapting to this force. If a dog runs off, with me left holding the lead, first, my forearm will extend to the tug of the lead, next, my shoulder will follow. Depending on my strength and the size of the dog, the movement will continue until my whole body has responded in some way—either by halting the dog or losing balance, falling forward and being dragged along by the dog.

Although my body is acting, it should appear to be reacting—a difficult task. Any isolation exercise will help to get one part of the body moving whilst others stay still. This is an essential mime skill. Simply isolate various parts of the body and move them independently to all other parts.

The next step is a little more difficult. Choose a part of the body and imagine a piece of string attached to the part—a piece that is attached to a fixed point and becoming progressively shorter. You will be dragged with the impulse acting upon various parts of your body—toe, heel, nose, navel, knee etc.

Next, try to clearly show the difference between hauling a rope and being dragged by a dog. Both are similar, but one is acting upon and the other is reacting to.

Characterisation. The life in any mime is not simply the mechanics of the actions but the comedy, pathos and personality of the piece. Constantly search for excuses for things to happen which require an emotional response. In fishing, for instance, the audience should be aware of how the performer feels about the day, the worm, the hooks, the river bank, tying knots, casting the line. Literally hundreds of things may go wrong before the hook actually lands in the water. The piece exists only through action, so the action must be interesting and constant. There is little point in sitting on a river bank for five minutes.

Make a list of things that can go wrong between getting up in the morning and leaving for school. Try acting some of them out.

ACTIVITIES

1 Start in a circle. No particular person leads. All must move together. As a sway or slight movement commences, the group must move as one. If the movements become complex, ensure that eye contact is not broken and that the movements are slow enough for everyone to stay together. The circle may be broken.

2 Four volunteers are chosen. Three leave the room and are ushered in one at a time to witness and repeat a mime. The group watches as the mime adapts to each individual's input and presentation.

(a) Coming home from school (how do you feel?), making a sandwich and drink (which?), and turning on the television (which show, how do you feel about it?).

(b) Catching a fish and losing it (which bait, how big?).

(c) Milking a cow (show its size and personality).

3 (a) Line up in groups of five. All face the back wall except the first member of each group. The teacher/leader performs a simple mime. First members tap second members who turn around and witness the mime performed by first members. The mime is then passed down the line. All groups witness as the last members perform the mime.

(b) First members invent their own mime. First and last are shown to all groups.

4 Gather in a circle, turn left; everyone facing the back of the person in front of them. One starts, front person is tapped and turns to watch mime. Taps next person to continue and so on. The mime is passed around the circle. How is it changed as it travels?

5 Two lines face each other, each person takes a partner. One group becomes an object and the others try to guess the object (whispering in partner's ear, not yelling out). As each pair finishes, they sit and watch the others. Remember, do not use the object, become it. If one method does not succeed, try another.

BEFORE AND AFTER

To be truly alive, a character must live in the minds of the audience before the character enters and after they leave the stage. Many good playwrights have used the technique of extensive build-up before a character enters. This allows flesh to be given to the character without any effort on the part of the actor. Two pivotal moments for an actor are the moment of entry and exit. They must seldom seem like a beginning or end—even at the beginning or end of a play.

Notice the technique of playwrights to have the lights come up or curtains open onto a scene rather than having characters enter an empty stage. This helps to create the impression that the audience is being allowed to glimpse an ongoing slice of life.

Research for a character must not only include what actually happens on stage but also what has happened before and what will happen after the time frame of the actual performance. This is not to say that clear answers and directions are provided for the audience. What is to happen may be left to each audience member to decide. However, an actor should have the answers to certain questions even though these answers may not be clearly shared with the audience. It is enough for the actor to know and flesh out the character accordingly.

ACTIVITIES

1 (a) Sandwich a short scene between a very solid entrance and exit. Try to have the scene totally dominated by what is about to happen and what has just occurred.

   (b) Try the same scene, changing only your entrance and exit. How does this influence the action?

   (c) Try the same scene but this time add ambiguous elements to the entrance and exit. Although not exactly stipulated, the possibilities must still remain strong.

2 Write a series of histories/pasts on separate pieces of paper (e.g. you have just had a tooth pulled, you are tired after a big day at the office). On other sheets write some futures/continuations (e.g. you have a successful career ahead, a murderer is waiting down the corridor, you will live happily ever after). Characters choose one history and future and enter a basic improvisation scene (bus stop, restaurant etc.). The aim is, as clearly as possible, to spell out the past and future without allowing these to dominate the present.

VOICE

However much an actor attempts to augment character with other details, the principal mode of expression will usually remain the voice. Voice is central to the actor's being. Key words or phrases may be crucial to the creation of a character. Mannerisms of speech such as 'Ah', 'Um' or 'y'know' may also provide a key to character.

It is as important for an actor to make use of projection and train the voice as it is for a dancer to train the body or a musician to practise an instrument. Untrained actors, dancers and musicians are capable of high degrees of artistry. Ultimately, however, all three disciplines are based on a combination of skill and creativity. Artistry is seldom achieved by one alone.

ACTIVITIES

1 (a) Imagine the voice as a musical instrument. From television or live, listen to the sounds of someone speaking or reciting a speech but ignore the meaning that the words are portraying. Think only in terms of:

- pitch (high or low)
- speed (fast or slow)
- rhythm (regular or irregular)
- timbre (tone)
- emotive quality (mood and feeling)

just as you would with a piece of music. Now, reproduce these elements using your own voice. Read a speech or passage from the newspaper; make up your own words. Meaning does not matter—reproduce only the manner of delivery.

(b) Next, repeat the passage, altering only one of the five stipulated elements. Be careful not to allow the change to significantly alter the other elements, e.g. a slow passage must remain slow even though the pitch may rise. The quality you may have most difficulty in controlling is maintaining a constancy of emotion. Continue the exercise attempting to change only one element at a time whilst maintaining all other elements:

- Which combinations are most difficult?
- Are there impossible combinations?
- Which combinations are most effective?
- How much is emotional quality a predetermined element and how much a product of the combination of the other elements?

2 Using only words or sounds and the qualities of your voice, attempt to recreate the essence of one of your favourite pieces of music. Avoid allowing the meaning of your words to dominate your method of delivery. Also avoid use of musical phrases or exact elements from the music. Your task is to find analogies and vocal elements, not sing or hum.

3 Listen to someone's normal speech pattern. The five stated elements may be extremely subtle with one or two elements predominating. When you have determined the predominant elements, exaggerate only these elements out of all proportion.

   Now, make a decision in relation to all five elements and exaggerate the qualities you perceive them to have. Once your exaggeration is established, start to bring each element back to a more natural level.

   How exactly can you reproduce the initial voice?

4 Choose a random selection of the five elements and create a voice from them:

   - Add movement/gesture.
   - Decide a background for the characters.
   - Provide thought/motivation for the actions.

   Write a short monologue and bring all of these elements into play.

INNER PULSE

Every character has a speed and rhythm. A late commuter will move at a different pace and in a different manner to a relaxed barman.

ACTIVITIES

1 Use some rhythm sticks to create the speed and rhythm of the following:
   (a) a postal worker
   (b) a factory worker
   (c) a dock worker
   (d) a teacher
   (e) a doctor
   (f) a typist
   (g) an office worker

> (h) a stressed shopkeeper
> (i) a disillusioned teenager
> (j) a disco king/queen.
>
> Invent your own suitably rhythmed occupation.
>
> Now deliver a speech from one of the characters with the rhythm playing in the background.
>
> 2 Choose a character who you believe has a strong rhythmic quality. With a pair of rhythm sticks, walk around the room using the pulse from the character to help determine some of the characteristic role qualities. A speedy, short, sharp pulse may create finnicky, staccato movements and gestures. Conversely, a strong and slow rhythmic pattern may create a character with great inner or physical strength.
>
> Once the rhythm/pulse is firmly established, put down your rhythm sticks and try to feel that character's inner pulse. Attempt a scene placing characters of similar and contrasting rhythms/pulses together. Which scenes work best?
>
> 3 Choose a passage from a play that has a strong rhythmic quality. Shakespeare is ideal for this. Create a character based primarily on the rhythm of the passage. How difficult is this to achieve successfully?
>
> 4 Choose a passage from a play that has little inherent rhythm. Determine a rhythm/pulse for the character. Have the character deliver the passage with the pulse being played on rhythm sticks in the background. Try a contrasting rhythm. How does this affect the delivery and perception of the passage?

SELF

Actors are often asked how much of their personality is invested in the role that they are playing. The answer is always the same—some of them. It is almost impossible for actors to play characters who they can't relate to or don't understand. Actors put their character together from the bits and pieces that they research, and some details which come from their own experience. Actors often play the 'what if' game. 'What would the character do if . . .?' This often becomes simply 'What would I do if . . .?' The 'what ifs' don't have to come from the play that is being acted. 'What ifs' help an actor to flesh out the character and help the audience to imagine the character as having a life before and after the actual time of the play.

ACTIVITIES

1 If you were to act these characters, what personal qualities would you be able to draw on?
   (a) a member of the clergy
   (b) a police officer
   (c) a lover
   (d) a monster
   (e) a baddie
   (f) a knight or lady of the Round Table
   (g) a king or queen.
2 How do you see yourself? Who/what would you be if you were one of these characters?
   (a) one of the seven dwarves
   (b) a character from the Arthurian legend
   (c) a car
   (d) a piece of fruit
   (e) a Hollywood legend
   (f) a character from history
   (g) a Greek god
   (h) a character from the Bible
   (i) a character from the Dreamtime
   (j) a character from Shakespeare
   (k) a comic book hero.
3 Make a list of famous characters who you believe are most similar to you as a person. Make a list of those who are most dissimilar. Do the lists tell you anything about how you see yourself?

THE QUESTIONS AN ACTOR MUST ANSWER

Invent a character and situation and answer the following questions.

1 Who am I?
   What is my age? _____
   What is my sex? _____
   What do I do? _____

2 How do I look?

What is my height? _____
What is my weight? _____
How do I carry myself? _____

3 How do I feel?

... at this moment _____
... about the past _____
... about the future _____

4 Where am I?

Am I inside or outside? _____
Am I alone? _____
Am I safe or in jeopardy? _____

5 What time is it?

What century, year, month and hour? _____
What season? _____
Am I late, early or on time? _____

6 What is around me?

What people, if any? _____
What objects/furniture? _____
What atmosphere (weather, fog, mood)? _____

7 What is happening?

What am I and others doing? _____
What have I just done? _____
What will I do next? _____

8 What are my relationships?

How do I feel about specific people? _____
How do I feel about people generally? _____
How do I feel about life in general? _____

9 What do I want?

What is my immediate aim (objective)? _____
What is my overall aim (super-objective)? _____

Examples:
(a) Police officer at the scene of a robbery.

- objective (immediate aim): to get a robber out of a bank
- super-objective (overall aim): to stay alive to collect the pension.

(b) Cook first day on the job.
- objective: to get the pancake mix off the ceiling without the chef noticing
- super-objective: to hang on to the job and become a great chef.

(c) Seventy-year-old at home.
- objective: to make a cup of tea without spilling it
- super-objective: to prove independence and avoid being put in a home.

II
ON STAGE

4
THE DIRECTOR

'I would undertake to teach anyone all that I know about theatre rules and technique in a few hours. The rest is practice.'

Peter Brook

The director's prime role is to make sense of the script. It is the director's understanding of the scripted material which will ultimately shape the performance.

The director coordinates and utilises the skills and assistance of the entire theatrical team. The director is the fulcrum upon which the creative machine is balanced.

THE DIRECTOR'S COMMANDMENTS

1 Directors should enjoy working with groups and individuals.
   Recluses generally make very poor directors. Maintain some aloofness to garner respect, by all means, but avoid being inaccessible and locked away.
2 Directors should know how to lead.
   Persuasion without bullying, and respect without fear or resentment should be the aim of the director. Actors look for and require direction.
3 Directors should prepare.
   Some interpretation or impression of role or script is required at the start of each rehearsal—including the first. Not all cast members appreciate total freedom to explore at rehearsals—especially if it is the director rather than the actors exploring. Know the script inti-

mately and be prepared with appropriate directions and suggested activities. Actors should take your lead primarily because they have confidence in your knowledge of the script.

4 Directors should be flexible.
Although the director should offer clear directions regarding role, interpretation and blocking, contributions from the cast should not be ignored. Delivered at the appropriate time and in the right spirit, cast suggestions can and should be an invaluable source of ideas.

5 Directors should be decisive.
The last word is always the director's.

6 Directors should be clear.
Directors should avoid offering too much information in a single session or instructions that are unduly complicated. The rehearsal process is just that—a process. Complicated instructions or concepts should be divided into steps and introduced over a number of rehearsals. Do not expect opening night perfection in the first rehearsals. Character building is part of the process—not an immediate outcome of the first rehearsal.

7 Directors should be consistent.
Ideas, blocking and interpretation that apply to one rehearsal should also apply to the next. The rehearsal process should be a gradual and logical development rather than series of lurches from one idea to another. Maintain constant communication with the stage manager to ensure that directions are being recorded accurately and maintained for each rehearsal.

8 Directors should avoid acting.
Actors should be given credit for being able to interpret instructions. Directors should avoid saying, 'like this'; this withdraws any sense of ownership from the actors. The play may belong primarily to the director, but the role should belong to the actor.

9 Directors should be tactful.
Directing through a megaphone, or making public speeches with information that could be delivered in private, are not endearing directorial qualities. Dealing with people is at the heart of the director's role. Directors should know the actors and how to assist them to produce their best work. Each actor will respond individually—be aware of and prepared for this.

10 Directors should be positive.
Criticism is a poor way of developing confidence. Confident voices are louder and confident characters stronger. All criticism should be constructive and praise offered where possible.

11 Directors should be organised.
The limited time available means that it must be scheduled care-

fully. A balance is required between rehearsals with and without scripts, workshops with and without scripts, discussion and technical considerations. Directors should avoid spending too much time:

- on sets or technical considerations to the detriment of the cast
- on blocking rather than delivery
- with one or two individuals
- on workshops without script
- on script without workshops
- on the opening scenes.

Amateur productions are notorious for openings which suggest great promise but which deteriorate into dreary second acts and virtually non-rehearsed curtain calls.

12 Directors should delegate.
The director cannot be totally involved in all areas at all rehearsals. The stage manager absorbs much of the director's load, but other clear roles of responsibility should be established. A person to receive simple enquiries and pass them on to the director at the appropriate time could prove most helpful. Large casts may burden the director with such a copious amount of questions that information overload inhibits the director's ability to be creative. Directors need space and time to think.

13 Directors should appreciate.
Many small jobs will be going on around the director; each one vitally important to the person(s) involved. The director should be aware of and appropriately acknowledge all contributions offered towards the performance.

14 Directors should believe in discovery.
Directors should tend towards knowing what they don't want more than exactly what it is that they require. Actors should be allowed the luxury of believing that they have discovered and created a part for themselves rather than having had it thrust upon them.

BLOCKING

Blocking is positioning and movement on stage. It is important to rehearse in a space equivalent to your theatre space so that blocking may start from the first rehearsals. Allow blocking to come from the lines rather than participate in too much pre-planning. In some scripts, there are literally hundreds of positions and moves. It is best to see what looks most natural before deciding the blocking; although the compli-

What does the blocking say about the relationships between the characters?
(Les Liaisons Dangereuses *by Christopher Hampton. Directed by Roger Hodgman; designed by Tony Tripp. Photo courtesy Melbourne Theatre Company.)*

cated movements of large casts may require some working out on paper before a rehearsal commences.

It is possible to correctly block a single scene in a number of different ways. It is often not a case of being right or wrong, but of being most appropriate for your aims. Once, it was considered bad form for actors to sit down, to cross legs or even to turn sideways on stage. Directors who wish to produce a completely authentic piece of theatre may do well to search out the conventions which governed during particular periods. Today's conventions are generally common sense guidelines:

- If actors turn their backs while delivering lines, they may not be heard.
- If actors deliver lines from behind other actors, they may not be seen.
- If actors stand stationary for too long, they may appear uncomfortable and artificial.
- If actors move around too much, they may upset audience concentration.
- If actors stand in lines, circles or semi-circles, the effect created may seem artificial.
- Actors who move while others are delivering lines may be distracting.

THE DIRECTOR

Blocking is like lighting—if the audience notices it, it is not doing its proper job. Blocking should give actors the opportunity to deliver lines in the most comfortable and appropriate position while allowing the audience the best hearing and viewing access.

Self-blocking is an excellent exercise for actors. Some directors commonly do not tell their actors where to go on stage. During each performance, they are required to make new choices of how to make a scene. Actors in such circumstances are required to be extremely sensitive to each other's moves. Inexperienced directors may gain much from watching actors struggle to block their own scenes. From the vantage point of audience, the most appropriate and inappropriate blocking may become clear and some of these ideas may be worth incorporating.

The director plays the equivalent role of both film editor and director. A film may easily proceed from far shot to medium to close-up. Once the film is shot by the director, the editor splices the raw footage to specifically focus the audience's attention. The theatre director focuses audience attention primarily through blocking.

Example

Storyline—A couple argue at a large party. One slaps the other.

Film—Shot 1—Far shot of party.
      Shot 2—Medium shot of couple arguing.
      Shot 3—Close-up of hand striking face.

Theatre—A couple mingle in the large crowd at a party (far shot). Above the din of the party, the sound of their raised voices is heard. They move to a position of significance and/or the attention of the party becomes focused on them (medium shot). The guests are shocked as the hand strikes the face (close-up).

Although the audience has the option of viewing any area of the stage, the director has focused their attention onto the stage as a whole or a particular part of it. Just as a film requires a variety of shots to be considered interesting, so a theatre piece must show variety in blocking and focus.

ACTIVITIES

Blocking

1 Choose a script segment with at least three characters and a number of entrances and exits. Ask your actors to block the scene

with as little input from yourself as possible. Ask them to remember these guidelines:

- Avoid being too static—some movement must occur.
- Avoid shunting—everyone playing trains and moving around in different directions.
- Avoid wandering—moving for no reason.
- Avoid masking—standing directly in front of another actor.
- Avoid upstaging—taking focus from an actor who should have it, or standing so far upstage that the downstage actor is forced to face away from the audience.
- Avoid pretty patterns—straight lines, circles, squares and semicircles all have their place on stage but are seldom seen in real life.

After watching the actors attempt the scene a number of times, choose the best of their efforts and block the scene to your own taste.

2 Using blocking rather than facial expressions complete the following exercises:
   (a) Show a conflict between characters 1 and 2. How does character 3 react?
   (b) Show that the three characters are close friends.
   (c) Show that character 1 is angry with characters 2 and 3.
   (d) Show that the characters all share a secret.
   (e) Show that characters 1 and 3 are friends and that 2 is not part of this friendship.
   (f) Show, in turn, that each character is the strongest/weakest. In how many ways is this possible?

   It may help to give each of the characters a simple line to say. The line should not be significant, and should be the same for each situation.

Focus

1 The actors improvise their own scene. As soon as the actors seem comfortable in one configuration, have them change the focus of attention. First and foremost, someone must have the major focus at any particular moment. This actor must not only take this focus (by action or word), but all other actors must be willing to give focus. Provide a reason for the focus to be altered and attempt to have the changes proceed as smoothly as possible. When the actors have mastered giving focus to people, ask them to give focus to objects (such as a chair or table) or spaces (such as a doorway).

2 Create a public place (bar, bus stop, football match, shopping centre, workplace) with at least twenty actors. Set the scene first with the expected din and pandemonium. Once the scene is set, groups and individuals must attempt to take focus. Others in the group must be willing to give focus for this to work. The imaginary audience should be able to clearly see and hear the person(s) taking focus. Focus should travel from one group to another.

Once the group has accomplished this, have the director take over as a kind of conductor. Although the characters continue to play throughout the scene, they gain or lose focus as the director points to or away from them. The director should invent signals to denote the exact amount of focus required. Remember, groups must be willing to offer as well as take focus.

3 One character enters a space and attempts to hold attention centre stage. This person represents the 'protagonist'—the character making a speech or demanding audience attention. No words are said, but stance (including sitting or lying down) demands focus.

This character may try a number of different stances; making use of arms, legs or facial expressions before finding one that is comfortable and attention-getting. When this character is finally established, a second character enters and attempts to take the focus from the first character.

The second character may try a number of stage positions:

(a) upstage
(b) downstage
(c) stage right
(d) stage left
(e) stationary
(f) moving
(g) no limitations.

Which was the most effective in taking attention from the main character?

4 Try the same exercise with the first character allowed to change position to 'challenge' the second character. The first character may move from centre stage. Both may move at will. They should avoid touching.

5 Choose two teams. Dress or identify the teams differently. This may be sleeves up/down, jumpers on/off, hats on/off or an identifying colour or ribbon. As a group, each team attempts to win the audience's attention. Sound and movement are permitted but the sounds should not be a contest of loudness.

6 This time, send on each character one at a time—one from team

Light tops versus dark in the battle of focus. Who is winning?

1 followed by one from team 2. Audience members may vote after each entry as to who is winning their attention.

7 Add various furniture settings. Allow some characters to use masks or costumes.

Balance

1 Instead of having the two characters compete for attention, have them move to complement each other, i.e. to balance the stage.

2 This time, instead of allowing character 1 to move from centre stage, a third character is added to balance the second character. That is, character 1 establishes a balanced stage, character 2 offsets the balance and character 3 re-establishes the balance. Remember that centre stage is an area rather than a fixed spot. Off-centre may be a stronger position than dead-centre.

3 Sending on one character at a time, see how many characters may enter a scene and maintain the balance. At a given moment, send in a character to upset the balance. This may be accomplished by position, movement or stance.

VOICE

Projection is part of the actor's art. Directors should have an understanding of vocal techniques and projection. Many books are available on the subject. In the simplest terms they suggest:

- stand up
- keep the head up
- face the front
- fill the lungs
- use the chest and head for depth and resonance
- control the breath.

Yelling is not projecting and actors who are straining are doing something wrong. There are no small voices, only poor projection. Should you be working in a large auditorium or with an actor who has a difficult or extensive role, it is good idea to allow a decreased volume for rehearsals. This will limit the strain on voices. There are some simple techniques which will help the inexperienced:

- Exaggerate their roles to make them larger than required. Bigger characters use bigger voices. It is a far simpler task to pull back an exaggerated character than to draw out an introverted one.
- Avoid complicated movements which may inhibit the actors because so much concentration is required.
- Large open gestures will assist some characters to feel less constrained vocally.
- Always project to the furthest wall, or even past it. Should you have the luxury of rehearsing in your theatre space, the furthest seat from the stage should become the focus of all voices. If voices are still inadequate, try projecting three metres past the furthest seat.
- If actors are talking too fast, get them to do things. This should slow their pace. As an exercise, ask them to describe drawing slow circles in the air.
- Memorise a short speech. The speech is to be delivered in two ways:

    (a) with as little action as possible

    (b) with considerably more action.

    Note the differences. As the amount of action increases, the pace of speech generally slows down. Actors who rush through lines may be slowed considerably by having something to do as they deliver the line.

- Specific actions may assist some actors who are delivering without emotion. 'Doing' may help their 'feeling'.
- Actors delivering slabs of meaningless words may be asked to paraphrase the meaning or improvise. Paraphrasing and improvising will also assist actors having difficulty remembering lines. Lines are more easily learned as meaning than as single words.

- It is no coincidence that actors reading from script or unsure of their lines tend to project poorly. Lines should be learned and scripts dropped at the earliest possible date. Alternatively, paraphrase initially and return to the exact wording when projection, role and meaning are established.
- As a warm-up before any script reading or vocal work, run through all of the vowels preceeded by the consonants: a e i o u; ba be bi bo bu; ca ce ci co cu; etc.

SCRIPT

APPROACHING A SCRIPT

1 Read the script straight through; for understanding, as literature and for pure enjoyment. Do not get side-tracked into thinking about too many details or the mechanics of producing the script.

- What is the basic plot or storyline?
- What are the subplots?

2 Read the script again and start to uncover and note further depth that may exist.

- What sections have lesser and greater emotional importance?
- What are the crisis points?
- What aesthetic values are in evidence?
  visual—the look of the piece
  aural—the sound of the language, speech rhythms
  intellectual—values, philosophies, ideas, themes

3 Read the script a number of times, taking a different character's point of view each time.

- Is there a protagonist? antagonist?
- Which characters have greater and lesser importance?
- Which characters develop or learn and which remain static?
- Which characters are symbolic or representational, i.e. they stand for or in place of something?
- What relationships exist between characters?
- What pressures are exerted on characters and how does each react?

4 Start to make choices—especially where the playwright has been ambiguous or open-ended information is offered.

- What happens before and after the action of the script?
- What is each character's history?
- What is the basic theme, i.e. what is the play saying?

THE DIRECTOR

- What symbols exist—characters, action, setting, speeches?
- What are the answers to the script's perplexing questions? (Should the director not choose to offer solutions, this becomes the director's statement—'There are no easy solutions'.)
- What motivates each character's actions? How should each react in particular circumstances?

5 Decide what you think the script is saying. Determine what you want to say through the script, and how you can best achieve this.
6 Decide what styles of presentation and acting will be used.

- abstract, realistic, naturalistic, stylistic, symbolic, exaggerated, comedic, tragic.

7 Start to develop some overall concepts of staging, blocking and the mechanics of the production.

- How should it look?
- How may certain scenes be staged?
- What is possible?

DIFFICULT AND WORDY PASSAGES

Ask actors to complete the following:

1 Underline the minimum essential words required to deliver the passage and still retain meaning. Concentrate on verbs and nouns. Consider that basic meaning is less likely to be found in adjectives and adverbs than verbs. Coarse actors are notorious for stressing adjectives whilst ignoring the basic meaning of a sentence. Deliver the passage using only the underlined words.
2 Walk around and deliver the passage bouncing a ball. The ball is bounced only on the essential words or words which require stress. The bouncing not only reinforces the stress, but provides a pause after the word.
3 Continue the bouncing procedure adding low and high bounces and 'throw and catch'. This provides at least three levels of stress. The ball may be used rhythmically or to establish pauses. This is especially effective for actors who choose to ignore commas and full stops or who treat commas and full stops as identical pauses. Try one or a low bounce for commas and two or a high bounce for full stops. This adds nothing to the emotional content of a passage, but it makes it much easier for the reader and audience to follow.

After some practice, if the actor still requires pressure to pause, the bouncing ball may be imagined. Hopefully, by opening night, the actor will be concentrating on the meaning of the passage far more than bouncing balls.

4 Divide the piece into words that are to be unstressed, stressed and very stressed. Think of language in the same way as music. Variations in stress may be achieved with changes to speed, pitch, volume, tone or attack.

A musician must isolate and stress the melody from the chords and passing notes. An actor follows a similar process—identifying and dividing essential meaning from flowery description.

ACTIVITIES—SCRIPT INTERPRETATION

Group interpretation

Form a circle with a maximum of twelve individuals. The group attempts to give meaning to a difficult sentence or phrase—one which may be causing some difficulty in rehearsal. Each person adds only one word as the sentence proceeds around the circle. Allow a number of revolutions. Each individual word and pause will be given particular significance, but groups should strive for a common group delivery and interpretation.

Style

Read a passage of script as if:

- arguing over a restaurant bill
- making a point in a debate
- delivering a political speech
- delivering a lecture
- reading the news
- telling a lie
- pleading for mercy
- sentencing a criminal
- telling a joke
- telling a bed-time story
- commentating at a sporting event.

Significance

No matter how essential a playwright may feel, the final arbiter of success lies with the relationship of actor and audience. The script is a mere vehicle for emotion; it is not the emotion itself. Similarly, a piece of musical manuscript, although potentially moving, is not inherently moving; it is a piece of paper covered with dots. In the right hands, it may prove to be profoundly moving. Lacking the right musician and instrument, it is less than inspiring.

The significance of a passage may be as determined by the actor and the context as by the content of the passage. As an example, let us take the blandest of scripts—the telephone directory.

(a) An actor reads from the directory a list of schools. Gauge delivery and audience response. Next, the actor reads the list as if the schools were those which have been short-listed for closing. Once again, gauge delivery and response. As a further development, the audience is asked to take the role of interested parents or students. Gauge how this affects delivery and response.

In each case, the script has not altered, but the context has contributed to the delivery of the actor and the response of the audience.

(b) Try the same exercise, again using a list of names from the phone book. Determine a context which involves both the reader and audience. The context may range from something dramatic, such as a list of war dead, to say, a list of scholarship winners.

An appropriate pause will be required after each name, reflecting the amount of significance given to each. Mere names in some circumstances may take on profound meaning as the audience recognises each one as a human being rather than a mere statistic. Both reader and audience breathe life into the names so that the list becomes more than mere words.

Other arts

Art, music, drama, dance and visual arts are divided more by practicality than intention. All are interrelated. Each tries to communicate emotion and meaning. The differences lie in how they go about it.

With this in mind, it is possible to use one art form to interpret or gain entry into another. If a passage is proving impossible to interpret as mere words, try using another form to give it meaning. For example, colours have emotional overtones. Your passage may suggest a colour which could provide you with a hook into its emotional meaning. The right piece of music played before or during a speech may provide the actor with an understanding of complex emotional overtones which would be impossible to explain verbally. A painting or photograph may provide the same understanding.

To show how music may provide an emotional backdrop to a piece, try this exercise.

Three contrasting pieces of music are chosen. They are to be played one at a time under a passage, which is to be read. They should be spliced together or quickly changed from one to another. The reader cannot help but be influenced by the music for, as well as influencing the basic delivery, it provides the emotional backdrop for the audience.

Try this passage as your basis of musical experiment. The entire passage may be read a number of times; each with a different musical backdrop, or the music may change part-way through.

> The last time I saw Fiona, she was beside herself. Her dress was caressing her thighs as the wind from the twin-engined jet cut swathes through her manicured hair. 'Don't go,' he whispered, 'I'll be lost without you'.
> The long hours of waiting had played tricks with his mind and reality had become a transient plaything. If she left, he would become an empty shell washed endlessly on the waves of infinity—a broken toy of wind and water; caught forever in the twin golden twilights of sunshine and sand.
>
> 'Don't go,' he called, his hand touching her shoulder. But his words were drowned by the screaming of an engine—too slow for take off; too fast for the body pushed blindly into its embrace.

Although the basic style approximates that of a failed Mills and Boon, with the right musical backdrop it may take on an entirely different complexion.

Try music that is:

- romantic
- horrifying
- light and frothy
- kiddie winkie
- heavy metal
- frenetic
- calm
- melancholy.

Subtext/supertext

The supertext is what you say; the subtext is what you actually mean. In one of its simplest forms, sarcasm, the supertext is the exact opposite of subtext. In more complicated versions, the simplest of supertexts may contain innumerable subtexts.

Supertext Person 1   Hello, how are you?
Subtext

Supertext Person 2   Oh, hi, fine thanks.
Subtext

Supertext Person 1   I haven't seen you for ages.
Subtext

Supertext Person 2   Yes, I know.
Subtext

(a) In pairs, read the lines straight.
(b) Write your own subtext.
(c) In fours, two read the supertext; two voices off provide the subtext.
(d) In pairs, read the supertext, using the subtext for meaning.
(e) Add a second subtext.
(f) What is the limit to the number of subtexts you can portray clearly?
(g) Provide a supertext and subtexts for the following:
- a girl and boy meet for the first time
- a teacher and parent on parent–teacher night
- an employer and job applicant
- an interviewer and interviewee on television.

Meaning

A piece of paper is passed around. Each group member contributes one line of script without reading previous entries. After each entry, the top of the page is folded over. Try to keep all entries on one side of a sheet, with a maximum of ten to fifteen contributions. Photocopy the results.

    The final script is to be presented by pairs who will try to make sense from the unrelated lines. Each pair may decide who will deliver each line. As a warm-up, or if the piece in its entirety is too difficult, groups may present two or more lines only.

    Try the same exercise in groups of five. One member will be the director and another the designer. Up to five actors may contribute, with a minimum of three.

Context

Have the group write a nondescript passage. Lines are to be delivered by one character. A second character provides only a non-verbal response. The passage should not be too prescriptive and should be open to many interpretations. Six to eight lines should suffice.

In pairs. Ask each pair to perform the piece, providing their own particular interpretive slant.

An example:

A It's getting darker
Pause. (Response or lack of from B)

A Are you afraid of the dark?
Pause

A A lot can happen.
Pause

A And does.
Pause

A There's no getting away from it.
Pause

A Your body sweats; your palms itch.
Pause

A I can't take it.
Pause

A Can you?
Pause

ACTIVITIES

Interpretation

1 Form groups of three. Each group writes a script for three characters—A, B and C. The script is to be as devoid of meaning as possible. There is to be a director and designer in each group. Scripts are swapped. Each group is to present their allotted script, offering their own individual interpretation. After the performance of all scripts, swap again. In how many ways is it possible to interpret a script.
2 Form groups of three to five. Each group performs a scene consisting entirely of lines from their favourite song or film.
3 Form groups of varying size, from pairs to very large. The script each group is to present is the Top Twenty for that par-

ticular week. Lists of any kind may become the basis of script interpretation.

Direction

In pairs. Each participant is directed by their partner to say one of the following lines:

>'I'm never coming here again.'

or

>'It's just not right, is it?'

Directors determine character, context and delivery. As each is performed, explore the relative strengths and weaknesses of blocking decisions.

A DIRECTING EXERCISE

Work initially in groups of three—a director, a designer and a scriptwriter.

The script is to be based on one of the following:

(a) A fairy tale
(b) A given situation
(c) A nursery rhyme
(d) A place
(e) A newspaper story
(f) Your choice

The style will be from the following list:

(a) A fairy tale
(b) News report
(c) Romance
(d) Fantasy
(e) Comedy
(f) Satire
(g) Tragedy
(h) Epic
(i) Detective
(j) Kung Fu

(k) Biblical

(l) Genre of your own

1. Choose a script and a style.
2. Determine three scenes—a beginning, middle and end. Characters must face a conflict or problem to be overcome and at least one character must learn or develop through the course of the encounter. There must be at least one protagonist with whom the audience will empathise.
3. Determine how many and what type of actor you require.
4. Write down as many details as possible of the style you have chosen:

   - What type of acting/character is required?
   - What type of dialogue is required?
   - What major incidents should occur?
   - What elements of the predictable and unpredictable are required?

   NB To set up the unpredictable, a strong predictable pattern must be set.

5. Determine a reason for the piece. What are you exploring? Why does the piece exist?
6. Experiment with setting. How does setting influence the piece?
7. Build into your piece something unpredictable for the actors—perhaps a scene where the outcome is unknown.
8. Hide something in the piece that the audience must look out for. Give them a reason to view the piece in detail.
9. Choose your actors and allow them to flesh out your piece:

   - Give them firm directions as to what is required of them.
   - Help them with delivery and presentation.
   - Position (block) them for the most successful and appropriate delivery.
   - Focus the action at all times.
   - Allow some freedom for individual initiative and input.
   - The designer takes responsibility for the look of the piece, the scriptwriter is responsible for the content, and everything else is the responsibility of the director and actors.

10. Making use of the same actors and similar script, change your choice of style.

5
THE DESIGNER

THE THREE STAGES OF DESIGN

The three stages of design:

1. Research and observation
2. Selection
3. Execution

are discussed in this section. Each stage is followed by activities.

1 RESEARCH AND OBSERVATION

It is important for designers to not only understand the details of the script at hand, but also to know where and when the script is set. If it is an historical piece, it is important for designers to research historical facts, such as what types of materials were used, what colours were predominant, and what kinds of furniture and eating and drinking utensils were used.

Depending on how detailed or how realistic the director wishes the production to be, the designer then decides how the details are to be used. Designers may not search for authentic accuracy; their prime consideration may be a representation of an overall feel or mood.

Their re-creation will be based on qualities such as line, shape and mass, space, texture and colour. These qualities will be explored with regard to unity and variety, balance, emphasis, rhythm, proportion and scale.

A re-creation may be much more than a simple copy. Just as playwrights draw from the real world and reorder details into another, greater reality, so the designer offers a version of reality which does more than merely represent. Designers may reflect like mirrors or stand apart and pass comment. The voice of the designer may be heard as loudly as that of the director or actors.

How details are presented depends on the designer's observation and understanding of contemporary audiences and the contemporary world. Plays are not put together like dinosaur bones in fossilised state. Plays must be dynamic, breathing entities which live with each presentation. Designers observe, comment on and ultimately reflect the age and society in which they live. They may research the past, but they observe the present and point towards the future.

A designer may be interested in the way a certain person dresses, how another parts their hair, or how furniture fits into a particular room. Designers live in a sensory world—collecting visual and tactile flotsam and jetsam, determining their emotional and psychological impact and reordering the pieces into a new and broader reality. Designers don't copy—they create.

ACTIVITIES

Space

1 With your eyes closed, how many questions can you answer about the details of the space that you are in?

- What colour is the ceiling?
- How many windows are there?
- What shapes are predominant?
- What adorns the walls?

2 Use a group of actors to create the following concepts in a theatre or open space:

(a) Crowded

(b) Empty

(c) Order

(d) Chaos.

3 Now arrange them in the following manner:

(a) To be viewed from above.

(b) To be viewed from one side.

(c) To be viewed from two sides.

(d) To be viewed from all around.

Cluttered and chaotic.
(Set model of the Melbourne Theatre Company production of Top End *by John Romeril. Directed by Paul Hampton; designed by Judith Cobb.)*

Ordered and open.
(Set model of the Melbourne Theatre Company production of The Tempest *by William Shakespeare. Directed by Gale Edwards; designed by Tony Tripp.)*

4 Create a space with as much/little width/depth as possible. Use props if these will assist.
5 Arrange a space to tell a story. You may use clothing, props and furniture but actors must be used as part of the setting rather than as characters.
6 Making use of minimum sets, costumes and props, improvise a scene in:
   (a) a lift
   (b) a football field
   (c) the capsule of a spaceship
   (d) an aeroplane
   (e) the cockpit of an aeroplane
   (f) the toilet of an aeroplane
   (g) a train
   (h) an art gallery
   (i) a picture theatre.
   Place the audience in the best position to view your design.
7 Form groups of five. Find an interesting space or area in which to work. Let the space dictate the nature of your performance. The space may be enhanced with some kind of decoration or change but the essence of the space must not be lost.

Observation

1 Without looking, try to give an accurate description of one person in your group. Describe hair, eyes, clothes—as many details as you know. Avoid descriptions that may offend the person. Can the rest of the group guess who you are describing?
2 Choose a partner and observe that person's appearance closely.
   - What does the hairstyle say about the person?
   - What does the clothing indicate?
     (a) One item is changed on each person without the other seeing. What is that item?
     (b) How many changes may be made whilst still maintaining the general appearance?
     (c) How few changes may be made to alter the appearance entirely?
     (d) Create an entirely different look for your partner.
     (e) Attempt to swap appearances.

(f) Choose one or two individuals to be completely changed by the rest of the group.
Try to create:

- an historical character
- someone you would meet on the street
- a fairy-tale character
- an occupation
- an animal
- a different personality.

Research

Work in groups of four. Arrange your group as if re-enacting a scene from history. Search for as many clues as possible to inform the audience of the period and incident. Avoid dialogue. If you lack adequate detail, do some research. Don't be concerned with acting, but concentrate on exactly how and where the characters will be situated. The statement should be made through design rather than character.

Line

1 Use large sheets of paper. Each member of the group signs their name with textas or large felt pens. To keep them relatively anonymous, the signatures are viewed upside down. Attempt to extrapolate some personality inferences from the line. Search for free and flowing curves, inhibited squiggles, show-off curls, angry dots and negative cross-throughs. Do not attempt accurate clinical analysis, you have no qualifications, but consider the quality of the line and the personality traits the lines tend to suggest.

What may you infer from these signatures?

They are not necessarily true of the person who has drawn the signature, but they do suggest that there is such a thing as personality of line.

2 Once the group has some understanding of the personality and quality of line, complete a signature for:

(a) a police officer

(b) a teacher

(c) a doctor

(d) a criminal

(e) an introverted wimp

(f) an extroverted boor.

3 In pairs. One creates a signature and the other a character from the signature. Swap.

4 Complete squiggles to suggest the following:

(a) Anger

(b) Excitement

(c) Calm

(d) Jealousy.

Strong horizontals.
(Portion of the set model of the Melbourne Theatre Company production of Rough Crossing *by Tom Stoppard. Directed by Babs Macmillan; designed by Richard Roberts.)*

Strong verticals.
(Portion of the set model of the Melbourne Theatre Company production of Hurly Burly. Directed by Gary Down; designed by Richard Roberts.)

Higgeldy piggledy lines.
(Portion of the set model of the Melbourne Theatre Company production of Lie of the Mind by Sam Shepard. Directed by Simon Phillips; designed by Judith Cobb.)

Which lines tended towards curves and which had angles? Which lines led down and which up? Which qualities were most common for each emotional state?

5 Use words or drawings to complete the following:

WHO	Line	Shape	Colour	Texture	Space
police officer					
teacher					
old man					
young girl					
dancer					

WHERE

desert
a palace
the bush
bus stop
supermarket

WHEN

early morning
midnight
midday
early evening
no time

WEATHER

windstorm
foggy night
frosty morning
hot day
snowing

Try to put together combinations of the above, e.g. a police officer in the desert in the early morning during a windstorm.

How difficult was it to find a consistency of design? Your selection will depend on what you make your primary focus.

The following notes on the design of The Three Sisters *set were provided by Hugh Colman.*

Line   Strong verticals to suggest both trees and the edge of a house.

Texture   A polished 'wooden' floor. A real tree branch. Gauze panels to evoke mist and distance.

Space   Use of almost the full stage to maximise the sense of outdoors after three Acts inside.

THE DESIGNER

Hugh Colman's design for The Three Sisters *by Anton Chekhov. (A State Theatre Company of South Australia production, from 1980.)*

How well do you feel the designer succeeded in achieving his aims? Could you suggest alternative methods of achieving the same effect or evoking the same mood?

Colour Muted autumnal browns to evoke that mood of a passing season.
Silhouette The trees against the sky. The furniture against the floor. The swing.

2 SELECTION

A designer's role is to offer selective information to the viewer. A designer works as a kind of editor—determining exactly which elements are required to establish character or setting. A character may be created with a scarf or hat; a setting may be established with a single prop or piece of scenery, such as a window or painting. This is the beauty and art of theatre—the expression of suggestion; the subtle nuance.

A designer may discover thousands of details about a play. From these, they must select those details which best suit the image they and the director wish to portray in the production. If too many details are chosen, the stage becomes cluttered; if too few, the setting may be lost. The fewer the details offered by a designer, the easier it will be to change from one scene to another. A chair designed like a box may later be used as a step; a bentwood chair, on the other hand, will always remain a bentwood chair.

An ideal stage design is one that does not 'box-in' the actors or clutter the stage to a great degree—unless this is the desired effect. Cutting corners may cost space but should produce a more pleasing design.

Amateur groups should leave as much to the imagination as possible. It is often better to have no sets than very poorly constructed and designed ones. These will tend to impede rather than assist the imagination of the audience.

In comparison to theatre, film and television maintain an insatiable appetite for realism. 'Location' or 'studio' seem to be the only choices, with both providing mere variations on the theme of reality.

The nature of theatre is such that no design may be truly realistic. Even a proscenium arch requires that the audience ignore the stage surround, the artificial lighting and other members of the audience. Although we are peeping into a room cut away on one side, it is still extremely artificial.

The audience accepts this lack of realism by embracing certain theatrical norms. A painted backdrop may not look entirely three-dimensional, but an audience will accept it as such. Of course, the right clues and directions must be given to the audience to assist this flight of imagination. Most theatre audience members will have no difficulty

In theatre, absolute reality is not required. We imagine that which is missing. (Set of the Melbourne Theatre Company production of Hedda Gabler *by Henrik Ibsen. Directed by Roger Hodgman; designed by Tony Tripp.) (Photo courtesy Melbourne Theatre Company.)*

filling in the missing pieces if, for instance, a window is suspended in mid-air rather than in a wall. For film and television, the wall is crucial to the suspension of disbelief.

With film and television, the editing is completed for the audience. No so in theatre, where the viewer is offered a greater choice of viewpoints and perspectives. It is the theatre designer's role to focus this attention and make it specific rather than general. A close-up of a chair may be impossible, but there are methods of drawing the attention of the entire audience to a chair. In theatre, the designer is the camera through which the audience peers. It is the role of the designer to determine which elements are essential and which will be assumed and imagined by the audience.

We have only recently come to fully appreciate the free-wheeling cinematic fast-cut nature of much of Shakespeare's writing. The absence of scenery in Elizabethan Theatre was one of its greatest strengths; a source of freedom rather than constraint. Scene after scene ran cinematographically; fast scenes, quickly edited—plot intercut with subplot—overt action with inner thought and turmoil.

Beware of extensive scene change times that place focus on the change rather than the action. Imagine the effect of running a film with a musical interlude placed between each change of setting. Err towards sparse scenery and rich action rather than the reverse.

In film, we are able to move from long shot to medium to close up

Keilor Heights High School Rock'n' Roll Eisteddfod performance at the Victorian Arts Centre. How have the designer and director attempted to focus our attention? Note the bold use of line.

YOU'RE ON

at will. In theatre, it is possible to move from outer to inner emotions, from actions to thoughts—a journey of infinitely richer terrain. The power of the play lies in its ability to simultaneously display all aspects of humankind—but, please, hold off the multitudinous array of scene changes between each aspect.

ACTIVITIES

1 Work in pairs. Think of a setting that you would like to create. Write down details of this setting. Choose the three most important details and try to create your scene using only things that you find in the room. Try not to use acting, even if people are used as part of the scene. Items that may not appear clear to the audience may be described to them, e.g. this piece of paper represents a window.

2 Now think of a character. Write down details of the character. Choose three details only and try to act out this character. See if the group can guess your character from the three details given.

3 Choose two completely different settings. Try to achieve a complete change from one scene to the other with minimum change of detail. For example, a table representing a bridge may become a doctor's office if a chair is added.

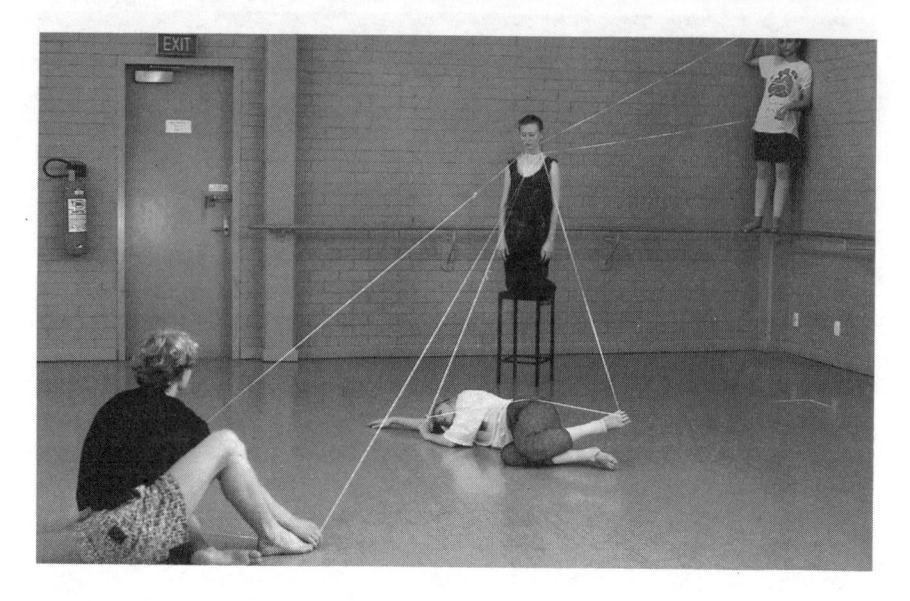

The elastic provides a visual representation of the invisible relationship between the actors, lighting and audience.

4 Work in groups of four. Each group chooses a simple item from the room, such as a pen or sticky tape. No other group should see the item. The group must then describe the item clearly enough for the other groups to guess what it is. Visual clues only; groups should not say what the item does or how it may be used—simply what it looks like.

5 Choose characters from a myth, legend or well-known story. Try to differentiate all of the characters from one, two or three design details only.

6 An actor stands in a space. Attached to various parts of the actor's body are about six lengths of looped elastic. The elastic lengths should be not less than 3–5 mm wide, 3–5 metres in length, and tied to make a loop. The loop is attached around the actor's arms, legs, torso, neck, knees, elbows or ankles. The elastic emanates away from the actor like the spokes of a wheel and is held by other actors. Experiment with the design possibilities of shape, focus and perspective.

(a) What is the effect of having the elastic emanating from one point on the actor's body?

(b) What is the effect of the actor moving stage left or right?

(c) What is the effect of moving some or all of those holding the elastic closer together?

(d) What is the effect of attaching the elastic to low and high points?

(e) What are the most effective shapes to create a larger or smaller actor, or larger or smaller space?

(f) Use the elastic as a method of determining the relationships of an actor to a space or set. It may be particularly helpful to experiment before a set has to be constructed. Extend the elastic from the actor to focused parts of set or furniture.

(g) To assist with decisions regarding the positioning of lighting and audience, use the elastic as if it were coming from lamps to the actor(s) or set.

(h) Attach the elastic to an upstage horizon point. Extend the elastic downstage left, centre and right. Place furniture and actors into appropriate spaces and on appropriate angles to reflect and exaggerate the perspective that is suggested.

3 EXECUTION

Once the choices have been made, the designer must decide how the desired effects may best be achieved. There are many practical considerations. Actors must move in their costumes, and sets and props must be able to be used as well as viewed. Some sets must tour, and size and weight are, therefore, critical. Costume materials have a certain feel, weight, fall, crease, texture and sheen. Sets must be stable. Scene changes must be accomplished quickly and efficiently.

Decisions are made in consultation with the director, with consideration given to the aims of the performance. A designer cannot simply decide that a box will double as a seat and a bed. The design must reflect the amount of realism that the director requires. Some directors have a clear vision and others are more willing to leave visual aspects to the discretion of the designer. There are as many ways to achieve the director's vision as there are designers.

Designers should have some understanding of perspective. By following and exaggerating the rules of perspective, greater depth may be added to flat backdrops, side walls and shallow stage areas.

If a horizon point is placed at some imaginary place at the rear of the stage (upstage), then all lines should have a tendency to proceed towards this point; floorboards or patterns on floors become thinner upstage and are directed towards the point; doorways and windows may be longer on the downstage (audience) side; side walls may be set

An example of limited raking-raising a platform above the level of the stage. Note how this assists the upstage actors. (The Sentimental Bloke, a musical written by Graeme Blundell, with music by George Dreyfuss. Designed by Richard Jeziorny. Photo courtesy Melbourne Theatre Company.)

so that upstage they are closer together. This exaggerates the audience focus and line of vision. Do not be afraid to exaggerate any perspective you wish to suggest. Although we normally expect 90 degree angles on windows and walls, we will readily accept the rules of perspective being exaggerated for dramatic effect.

Raking exaggerates the depth of the stage. A raked stage is one which is higher upstage than downstage. In fact, this is where the terms 'upstage' and 'downstage' originated. With the use of such a stage, actors upstage may compete more readily with those downstage. Adding height to the upstage areas may achieve a limited raking effect.

Although much favoured by amateur groups, open stages pose great difficulty for the designer. A common way to overcome the inherent problems is to limit the audience to two or three sides. In this way an upstage area is created. This assists the director and actors to choose a direction for delivery. The truly open stage allows no priority direction to be created. Sets require careful consideration so as not to mask the actors from any direction. Open stages are generally sparsely designed and directors often stylise both the design and the acting techniques when working in the round.

Colours contribute to mood, perspective and depth. Cool and less

How have perspective and sense of distance been exaggerated? Where is the horizon point? The buildings are browns and the cyclorama is bluish. (The Servant of Two Masters by Carlo Goldoni. Directed by Roger Hodgman; designed by Tony Tripp. Photo courtesy Melbourne Theatre Company.)

bright colours will tend to recede. The colours of the spectrum differ slightly for lighting. Rather than pure blue, red and yellow, lighting requires a greener yellow than normal to create a theoretical white light.

Colour combinations are essential to remember when lighting either sets or costume. Your sets and costumes will be lit by lights which will not only create shadow but may wash out the weaker colours. Red lighting may make the reds and blues seem quite startling, but the blue will appear quite purplish and any yellow will be orange rather than the pure colour that originally appeared on your set or costume.

When searching for appropriate colours, it is a useful technique to use floods or spots in a wash of three primary lighting colours: red, blue and yellow/green. You simply mix them until you feel you have the desired tone and search through your collection of colours or a catalogue for this tone.

If you are short of lighting but require a number of colour changes, it is possible, by using three primary lighting colours, to have virtually all colours of the spectrum available to you. It is extremely effective to light a cyclorama in this way.

Temperature, depth and height on stage are not only related to colour and to the differences between upstage and downstage. Because we read from left to right, stage right (audience left) is considered to be warmer and even, amazingly, higher than stage left. Characters walking from stage right to left appear to be walking downhill.

The effect is fractional and subconscious, but enough to establish status for a character who needs to take command of a stage. The place to do this is not upstage left—the coldest place on stage. In classical ballet, kings and queens are commonly found upstage left to make them seem cold and aloof—though not dominating. A mantel-piece or cherished photographs tend to be stage right and a menacing window or door, stage left.

This is by no means an unbroken rule or startling optical illusion—simply a tendency for us to wish to read and look from left (stage right) to right. It is more related to a designer's aesthetic choice than to any concept of right or wrong. Other cultures who read from right to left have the opposite reaction to ourselves.

Knowing this tendency, the designer and director are able to, say, place a hero generally more stage right than left; design warm interiors stage right and cool exteriors stage left; place entrances and exits involving temperature changes in appropriate places; have the hero losing a sword fight stage left (lower and colder) and finally being victorious stage right, or being tempted stage left and resisting temptation stage right.

As with all dynamic art, there are no unbroken rules; merely hunches, tendencies and taste.

THE DESIGNER

Ideally, a completed theatre design, far from being a necessary prerequisite for rehearsals, should be finalised as late as possible. The more professional the theatre company, the less possible this ideal tends to be. Obviously, directors must have something to work with at rehearsals. An ideal design is one which is loose enough to absorb the input of actors and the director as they commence the exploratory journey known as rehearsal.

A completed design with little room for input may prove stifling and, in extreme cases, inappropriate, to the final production. Actors and directors explore, experiment, discover, define, reject and refine; designers must be allowed the same luxury.

ACTIVITIES

1 Form groups of four—a director and three designers. Choose a space in the room and have a few props handy, such as chairs, a jumper and a bin. The director suggests three scenes and offers details of how the scenes will be acted. With a minimum amount of movements between scenes, the designers create three distinct scenes.

2 Form groups of five—a director, designer and three actors. The actors determine who and where they are and what happens; the director decides the style of production and the designer creates the look of the piece. As the actors walk through their lines, the director offers suggestions regarding acting, position (blocking) and presentation. The designer suggests ways in which this may be best achieved. There must be at least one scene change. Try the same piece with a different director and designer. Perform both pieces for the other groups.

3 In pairs—one directs and designs, the other acts. The actor has one line (from a famous play), a prop, one costume aspect and must make an entrance and exit. It must be clear who the character is, where they are going and have come from, and why.

4 Next time you watch television, divide the screen into upstage (background), downstage (foreground), stage left (screen right), stage right (screen left) and centre stage (centre screen). (I am only speaking figuratively—textas are not necessary!)

Flick through a number of shows over a one-hour period and monitor exactly where characters are positioned. In particular, monitor these formats:

(a) Drama—medium shot.

(b) One person talking and one listening—medium shot.

Belt
belt
Gloves
Check Skirt
Short laced boots
The Sentimental Bloke Tarts

Cloth cap
Knitted Vest
Belt
Striped pants
Wide cuffed pants
The Sentimental Bloke Larrikins

THE DESIGNER

(c) A talker—close-up.
(d) A listener—close-up.
(e) A romantic scene—screen position of the male as compared to the female.
(f) Interviewer—close-up and medium.
(g) Interviewee—close-up and medium.
(h) Party political broadcast.
(i) Situation comedy—medium shot and close-up.
(j) Nature show presenter.
(k) Talking heads.

Costume designs by Richard Jeziorny for The Sentimental Bloke. *Richard also designed the set. His notes on costume for the Melbourne Theatre Company production include the following:*

Parameters	Limited number of characters with multiple roles and therefore subdued costuming rather than bold statements. Evocative of period and social class; the Edwardian era in Melbourne before the First World War.
Line	Slightly scruffy to suggest the back streets of Melbourne.
Colours	Most important. To complement set. Burnt orange and gold, rich berry colours.
Texture	To look substantial. Wools, patterns, checks and stripes.

(l) A game show.
(m) A current affairs host.
(n) Advertisements.

- Is there a tendency towards one part of the screen? Can you determine why this might be?
- What effect is created by the various screen positionings and the choice of shot angle?

ACTIVITY

Design a series of costumes from this brief:
The play takes place in any capital city of Australia. Time, the present. The costumes must evoke a hopeless frustration which is engulfing everyone from yuppie executives to street kids. Society is in decay and materialism has replaced any sense of worth. One character can see through it all and has the answer, another thinks the end is close and wants to give it a help along, one survives in and on rubbish, one represents rebellion and another establishment.
Notes on set include:

Materials	Must establish the right context. Raw timber. Look-over-back-fence quality.
Line	Strong linear feel. Line moving in different directions.
Focus	Strong focus on playing area.
Colours	Boards dyed shades of warm tones. Cool blues as contrast.
Space	Open design to allow for many changing locations. Use of a 6 metre by 4 metre truck to allow for pre-setting and quick scene changes. (A truck is a small portable stage area.)

Design an open setting which, with minimum change, could be used for:

- a pub
- a battlefield
- a street
- and the interior of a house.

The set must suggest the period immediately after the Second World War.

A DESIGN MODEL—AN IMAGINATIVE APPROACH

Designing for the theatre is not so much a matter of drawing as of using space. Drawings, no matter how well completed, are exercises in two dimensions. It is always better for the amateur stage designer to create a scale model from the initial design.

Collect interesting shapes and materials for a model theatre. A shoe box will do nicely for the theatre, but a larger box would be better. In searching for interesting items carefully consider the following qualities:

Line	Is it straight or curved? Is it hard or soft in appearance? What do the lines suggest?
Direction	Does it move the eye in a particular way?
Shape	Is it regular? Is it realistic? Is it clearly defined? Is it static (stationary) or dynamic (suggesting movement)?
Proportion	What size is it? Does it tend to move back (recede) or come forward?
Texture	What does it feel like? Is it smooth or rough, hot or cold, regular or irregular?
Value	What are the most and least startling aspects? What particular qualities define the object and which are less important?
Mass	How substantial is it?
Colour	What effects of mood or image are created by the colour? How does colour relate to the above-mentioned qualities?

Suggestions for materials include wool, cotton spools and cotton, string, pieces of material of all kinds, tea towels, chains, hankies, plastic wrap, wood scraps, twigs, aluminium foil, leaves, flowers, doll's furniture, wire, cardboard, coloured paper, small toys, puppets, dolls and model figures (the smaller the better; make your own, if necessary), grass, sand, icy-pole sticks, matches, hoses, pieces of plastic, containers, carpet, underfelt, cotton wool and steel wool.

In groups of three or four, combine all of your materials and create a model theatre stage setting. Try to create a mood and feel rather than a particular place. For a city office, visual qualities are far more important than simply recreating a few desks. Don't forget sparseness in your overall design, if it is appropriate. Use coloured paper for designing backdrops or floor cloths and creating mood.

Designs by Graeme Base for flats of Scary Stories, a Victorian Arts Centre Art Ed production. Directed by Judith McGrath and featuring Drew Tingwell and Kate Whitbread.

With the addition of some exciting lighting by Ervin Kos, the flats are transformed from two dimensions into an atmospheric setting.

Once you feel you have your shapes and colours right, try adding some miniature figures which you could make out of cardboard. Next, if possible, use a torch, projector, portaflood, or electric light on a cord to see how shadows affect your design. Obviously, the darker the room the better. Try light from above, side, front and below. Which is the most effective? Cellophane over the light will help you to create coloured effects. If you do not have a portable light source, simply take your model over to the window and try it at different angles.

When your group is satisfied that they have created as strong a design as possible, ask the other groups to identify your group's intentions. Consider, in particular, these qualities and how they effect the overall design:

Rhythm   Repetition of line, shape or colour.
Harmony The blending of different shapes, textures or colour.
Unity   The drawing together of different elements to create a total or 'whole' impression.
Contrast The drawing together of disparate elements to make them clash.

Choose one design to make life-size and devise a suitable performance for the area. What problems are encountered in moving from miniature to life-size? Remember that there is no necessity to copy the smaller scale object exactly. Instead, attempt to reproduce its overall feel and mood, taking particular note of the qualities mentioned above. These qualities are the key to design control. Whether in large or small scale, if the qualities are similar, the impression should be identical.

A DESIGN MODEL—A MORE REALISTIC APPROACH

1 Choose a script you would like to produce.
2 Make a complete list of properties (props) and costumes. Decide which should be made, borrowed, bought, hired or created.
3 Decide on a set which will be suitable for the entire production. The simpler the set, the easier it will be to add something to allow it to be used as a number of settings. Decide on your style. Would it work best as a realistic box set (a room with the front wall missing as in a traditional proscenium arch), in the round or in another configuration? Should the audience be required to use imagination to a great degree? Would a two-dimensional painted backdrop be the most suitable method? Can slides and blank or mottled screens be employed? Is rear projection a possibility? Can gobos or special effects be used to change scenes? When you decide on your general set, determine how and where furniture will fit into the setting.
4 Using graph paper, draw three plans of your setting—aerial, from side-on and from the point(s) of view of the audience. Use a scale of 1:25 (or 1:20 if you would like it a little larger).

Richard Jeziorny with his model for the Melbourne Theatre Company production of Curse of the Werewolf.
(Photo courtesy the Victorian Arts Centre.)

THE DESIGNER

5 Using your aerial plan, divide your stage into nine equal areas. Place furniture as required. If different settings of furniture are required, you may find that scale cut-outs of furniture can be moved easily around on your plan. They need not be 3D models—merely cut-out shapes representing an aerial view. Keep them to scale.

6 When you are satisfied with your plan, it is time to turn it into a model—1:25 is again a suitable scale for this process. Cardboard is generally a suitable material, but three-ply, balsa or other easy-to-work-with material will create a more permanent model. Miniature pieces of furniture and actors may assist you to imagine how the final set will look. Make it as realistic as possible, complete with the right colours.

7 Using your aerial plan with the nine equal areas, decide on a lighting plot. Each of the six downstage areas will require two spotlights from an approximate 45-degree angle. Attempt to light from at least two grids of differing distance from the stage. If you are short of lights, you should concentrate on the areas that have most action or furniture. Ensure that floodlights cover areas not well serviced by spots. (See Chapter 7, 'Lighting', for details.)

8 When your lighting grid and model are complete, try placing your model under a window which has direct sunlight. Change the angle of the model to the light. If you have one, a portaflood or an electric light on a portable cord will give you a closer representation to stage lighting. Search for shadows, dark areas and areas which are too bland or too busy. This is where you will see the importance of an accurate scale model. Designs that do not appeal on a small scale will look no better when blown up to twenty-five times that original size.

9 It is now time to start work on your properties and costumes. Those to be built or made will require designing before the actual making process commences. Books on these processes are readily available. The initial design drawings need only be general outlines. Ensure that all design concepts are consistent with your overall theme. Remember that costumes (especially for dance) must be designed for moving as well as for looks.

10 To give the final check to your plans, lay out a room with furniture and other items to represent your setting. Do not guess scales. If your room is smaller than the stage to be used, reduce everything in scale. Never use an area that is larger than the stage you will be using. Even in large rooms, you should be able to isolate an area and thereby give the actors an idea of actual size. Ask some characters to read through—complete with movements—various short passages from your script.

After making final adjustments, you should be ready to consider budgeting for lights, sets, props and costumes and think seriously of turning your plans into more than mere ideas.

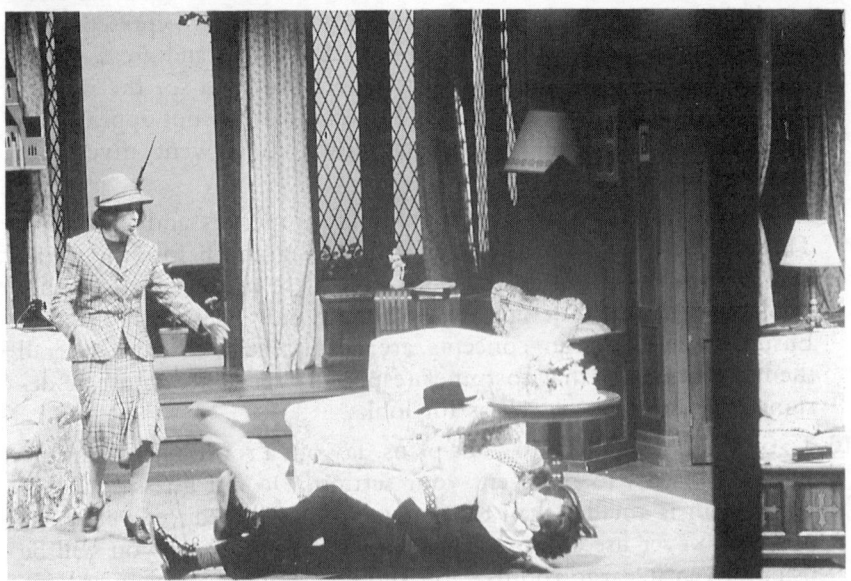

From set model to production.
See How They Run, *by Phillip King. Directed by Roger Hodgman and designed by Tony Tripp.*
(Photos courtesy Melbourne Theatre Company.)

6
BEHIND THE SCENES

THE STAGE MANAGER

The stage manager is responsible for the smooth running of rehearsals and the production. The stage manager lists and coordinates all cues. Performer movements, sound effects, lighting changes and musical cues are governed by the stage manager. Even rehearsal calls and the promptness of starting rehearsals and the performance are the responsibility of the stage manager. The stage manager accepts many of the organisational duties to ensure the director is free to concentrate more fully on the creative aspects of performance.

THE PERFORMANCE

All technical staff, lighting, sound and stage mechanics take their instruction directly from the stage manager. Using a prompt score or script, the stage manager, situated at a control desk, is positioned in prompt corner (PC)—normally to the left of the actors. The opposite corner is referred to as OP (opposite prompt).

The control desk, ideally, should be equipped with a headset and communications to all technical staff, dressing rooms and front of house.

'Ladies and gentlemen, this is your half-hour call' is usually the first call that a cast hears from a stage manager on the night of a performance. The stage manager then counts down all cues and entrances for the entire performance.

'Joan Roberts, five minutes please' is a signal to Joan Roberts that she has an entrance in five minutes.

Calls are of two types: 'Stand-by' or 'Get-ready' and 'Go'. An actor may require several minutes to move from the dressing rooms to the stage. A lighting technician may need as little as a few seconds if the lighting board is a modern computer-controlled type.

'Standby - LX Cue 1'
a few seconds
'Go LX Cue 1'

It is important for the stage manager to keep these instructions as clear and brief as possible.

Where there is no prompt desk with a communication system, the stage manager should be situated with the technical staff—in the lighting box or wherever, and an assistant appointed to supervise performers.

REHEARSALS

Prompt script

During rehearsals, the SM (stage manager) works from a prompt score or script. All moves, cues and prop requirements are entered on this script. The prompt script is put together from notes taken during rehearsal. A typical rehearsal notebook is created by placing alternating pages of script and blank pages into a ring binder.

The following is an actual stage manager's running plot used to call the 1985 Australian Ballet production of *Coppelia*. A full list of abbreviations and terms used, and explanation of some common theatre terms, follows the running plot.

FEBRUARY 1985

THE AUSTRALIAN BALLET

STAGE MANAGER'S RUNNING PLOT
Coppelia Act 1

Preset (Blackout)   Dome 1–51
     Act 1 Gauze in   2–51
                                                                              3–17

S/By House lights
      Curtain
      SWB Q's 1–5
      FLY Q1
      Dome 3 U.S.O.P. DR COPPELIUS—17
      Dome 1 U.S.O.P. House Door SWANILDA—51

Curtain up	Build into beginning of Mazurka
SWB Q 1 GO	Curtain halfway up
SWB Q 2 GO	Mazurka ending
SWB Q 3 GO (Build behind gauze)	Last five bars of Mazurka
FLY Q 1 GO	10 bars of music later
SWB Q 4 GO	Follow on
SWB Q 5 GO	Swanilda enters U.S.O.P
S/By Dome 2 D.S.O.P. FRANZ *ON CUE*	
Dome 2 PICK-UP	Franz with 2 peasant boys D.S.O.P.
S/By SWB Q 7 Dome 3 D.S.P. Door DR COPPELIUS Dome 1 U.S.C. SWANILDA (as she comes out of C.S. Double doors)	
SWB Q 7 GO	Franz staggers from balcony U.S.O.P (C.O.M)
S/By SWB Q 8	Dr Coppelius onto balcony
SWB Q 8 GO	Swanilda throws flowers at Franz D.S.P.

Abbreviations and terminology

Dome—followspot
1–51—followspot no. 1/colour no. 51
S/BY—standby
Go—execute cue
SWB—switchboard (lighting)
LX—lighting (In the Australian Ballet, SM's tend to call lighting 'Switchboard'. In theatre, opera, and music, SM's tend to call lighting 'LX'.)
FX—sound
Q-1—cue no. 1
Fly—to move suspended scenery (backcloths etc.) up and out of sight or down into view.
Flies—the area above the stage where scenery is suspended.
USOP—upstage opposite prompt
DSOP—downstage opposite prompt
USP—upstage prompt
DSP—downstage prompt
USC—upstage centre
DSC—downstage centre
CS—centre stage

```
|                 USOP          USC              USP            |
|                                                               |
| Wings   Opposite              CS           Prompt      Wings  |
|         prompt                             side               |
|                   Stage R.          Stage L.                  |
|                                 DSC                 Prompt    |
|         DSOP                                   DSP  corner    |
|                         ← Apron →                             |
```

                          Thrust
Audience   Audience

                          Audience

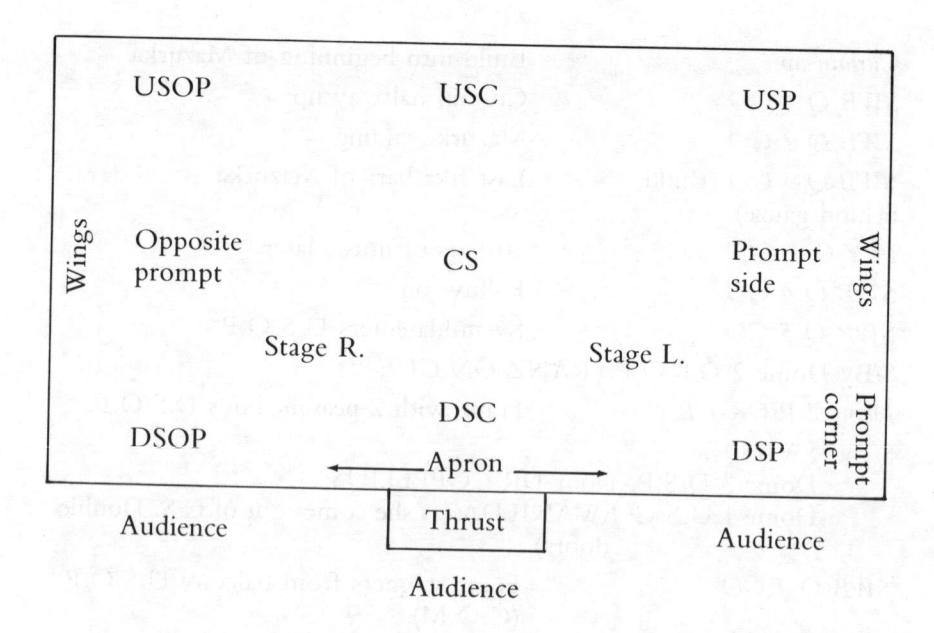

P and O/P—to an actor facing an audience, left is 'prompt' (p) and right is 'opposite prompt' (op). 'Prompt corner' is where the stage manager is usually set up.

Wings—The sides of the stage; out of sight of the audience.

Bump In/Out—moving a show in and out of a theatre.

Heads/Heads Up—warning signals when lights are being hung (rigged) and/or battens are being moved up and down.

Truck—a device on wheels that allows scenery to be moved easily. For instance, an entire dining setting may be set and trucked in and out in a matter of seconds.

Set—(short for setting) scenery

Schedule

The SM is responsible for drawing up a rehearsal schedule with the director. In drawing up the schedule, the SM should be aware of commitments of individual cast members. If a cast member has a single line in a scene, it may be unfair to include this member in the call. Some chorus members or those with small roles may, on the other hand, appreciate the opportunity to be involved in as many rehearsals as possible.

The SM should try to avoid situations where cast members wait around for extensive periods. The SM and the director have the responsibility of ensuring that all cast members have a clear idea of their commitments from the outset. It is also a wise director and SM who ensure that all cast members have an understanding of the performance as a whole—rather than simply the scenes in which they are involved.

It is the SM's responsibility to find out what props, costume or sets the director requires for rehearsals. This may involve scrounging old tables and chairs or finding suitable material so that actors or dancers may get used to working in long skirts. At this stage, these basic physical requirements are the responsibility of the SM.

The SM is also responsible for organising the rehearsal space. From a copy of the designer's plan (drawn to scale) the acting area may need to be taped out. Walls, doors, windows etc., that have not yet been made may need to be represented with coloured tape on the floor.

Following the instructions given by the director, the SM must take notes on everything that is likely to happen during performance—including blocking (stage positioning) and script changes.

'Bump-in,' and 'bump-out' are terms used to describe the process of setting up and 'striking' the show. In this task, the teams of mechanists and technical staff are coordinated by the SM. The SM also coordinates the technical rehearsal(s).

The quality of your stage management will be crucial to the success or failure of your show.

ACTIVITIES

1 Choose a segment of script which has plenty of action and at least one scene change.
2 Read the play as a whole to gain an overall impression. Read your segment, paying particular attention to details of stage management.
3 Mark the script with the following details:
   (a) lighting—general set-up, changes and special effects
   (b) blocking—character movements, entrances and exits
   (c) sound—amplification and special effects,
   (d) props—when required and where left after use
   (e) costume changes
   (f) set changes—flies, backdrops, trucks, pieces of scenery and furniture.

   Treat your segment as if it is an entire performance: half-hour call, house lights down, curtain up through to curtain calls and house lights up.
4 Underline all of your cues in two ways:

- Red—standby—allow adequate preparation time. (An actor may need time to walk from the dressing rooms, sound cues may take some finding etc.)
- Green—go—with the words or action that act as cues.

5 Draw up a separate plot for each of the areas listed in 3.

6 Draw up a prompt script from your individual plots. Make sure that you clearly and accurately note the relevant cues. If a word, say 'door', occurs a number of times, it is not appropriate to write:
   cue—Door
In most circumstances a phrase or sentence is better than a single word. Sometimes it may be more appropriate to use an action rather than a word cue.

7 Ask some friends to read your script aloud while you 'call' the show.

LIGHTING DEPARTMENT

A number of people with very specific roles combine to produce the lighting of a theatrical presentation. Firstly, the lighting designer, in consultation with the director and designer, determines an appropriate lighting design. Time of day, season, light source, shadow, style, desired effect, costume, make-up and set all require consideration.

Lighting must not only be adequate for visibility but suitable for the style of presentation desired by the director and designer.

The lighting designer draws a plan which is given to the lighting master, who coordinates the positioning, focus and colouring of lights.

In the theatre, there are three types of electricians—switchboard operators, follow-spot operators and stage electricians:

(a) Switchboard operators perform the actual lighting changes during rehearsal and performance.

(b) Follow-spot operators are known as 'domes' because they used to work in the dome of the ceiling. In England they are called 'limes' because of the 'limelight' that was once used. They work the follow spots during rehearsals and performances.

(c) Stage electricians hang, focus and change coloured filters in lamps, work dry-ice and smoke machines, pyrotechnics and effects (FX) of all kinds.

SOUND DEPARTMENT

Proper amplification and mixing of sound can be crucial to a performance. Extraneous noise must be minimised while music, sound FX, and voice must be picked up and amplified in the desired proportional mix.

Musical instruments may be acoustic or electrically amplified in a number of ways:

- through an individual amplifier
- mixed through the public address system (PA), or
- picked up by a contact microphone.

In most cases sound should be as 'natural' as possible and appear to come from an actual instrument or voice rather than from a speaker or wall.

The sound department in a professional theatre is an integral part of technical considerations. In consultation with the director and musical director, the sound department contributes to decisions relating to acoustics, amplification, prerecorded music and sound FX.

MECHANISTS

For the bump-in, mechanists are responsible for setting up scenery, flying (hanging) cloths and moving 'trucks' (sets on wheels). They must ensure scenery is set up safely and accurately, according to the specifications of the designer. Mechanists are also responsible for scene changes during the production. It is always advisable to time these before the dress rehearsal. The positioning of all scenery, tables and chairs should be carefully marked on the stage with coloured tape. Luminous tape may be used if (as is usually the case) changes occur on a darkened stage. In such cases, allow some working light. Don't expect changes to be made in total darkness. Practice is often necessary to achieve the desired change times. Special 'scene change' rehearsals may be required. Mechanists are also responsible for the bump-out, under the SM's supervision.

PROPS

Property personnel are responsible to the SM for the placement of props. Working from a plot provided by the SM, they will be responsible to ensure that all props are where they should be when required.

Props is short for 'properties'. These are the items which are used by the performers. They must be bought, built, borrowed or altered from existing props. These should be completed or acquired early enough for performers to be familiar with their use. A performer must know exactly where to find and leave a prop. Some performances utilise literally hundreds of props.

It is a good idea to lay out a map on a large table and always return props to the same position on the table. This plan of a prop table set-up is from the same Australian Ballet production of *Coppelia* referred to earlier.

FLOWERS Swanilda Act I Sc i	4 BEER MUGS Act II	3 LANTERNS Act II
DAGGER Dr Coppelius Act I Sc i	BOOK OF SPELLS Dr Coppelius Act II	4 CANDLES Act II
		6 WREATHS Act I Sc i
BASKET Swanilda Act I Sc i	LETTER Franz Act I Sc i	
		MAGIC WAND Dr Coppelius Act II

WARDROBE

As well as buying material to create entirely new costumes, this department may be required to alter existing costumes. The right costume must not only fit correctly but also allow for the performer's required movements and be relatively easy to maintain and clean. The upkeep and maintenance of costumes is a vital element in performances that have long production runs. If costumes are not available for the early rehearsals, substitutes must be found to help the performers imagine the feel and movement limitations of the costumes. Two performers may make use of the same costume by adding two sets of buttons or fasteners.

Remember that a quick change may be required for some performers. Velcro with false buttons may be the most appropriate choice for such circumstances.

COUNTDOWN TO OPENING NIGHT

SEQUENCE OF EVENTS FOR PROFESSIONAL THEATRE

Develop the idea.

Choose or commission the script or score.

Apply for the performing rights.

Determine the budget.

Book the venue.

Decide on the director, designer, musical director or choreographer.

Arrange for stage management and technical staff.

Organise the auditions.

Choose the cast.

Design the sets, costumes, lighting and sound. Build a model.

Arrange the first reading or run-through.

Commence rehearsals.

Organise advertising and marketing.

Open the box office.

Bump-in.

Re-rehearse on the stage itself—reblock movements.

Organise a full technical rehearsal.

Arrange a full dress rehearsal.

Opening night.

Your sequence will require some rearranging depending on your style of show. If you want to develop a script with your group, your first task will be to establish a working group. Decisions on budget, venue and script will then evolve from workshops. You may also find that, rather than isolate specific backstage roles, the performers will be involved in these areas. It also may be advisable to book your venue before you consider budget. This will leave less to estimation.

After your performance dates are set, it is always a good idea to make a schedule of anticipated completion dates.

Schedule	Completion date	
	Anticipated	*Actual*
Performers finalised		
Backstage and technical staff		
Theatre		
Budget		
Rehearsal schedule		
Script completed		
Script learned (no books)		
Choreography/music		
Designers commence		
Designs completed		
Model completed		
Sets commence		
Costumes commence		
Props commence		
Publicity printed		
Publicity distributed		
Tickets printed		
Box office opens		
Lighting		
Sound (FX)		
Props completed		
Costumes completed		
Sets completed		
Bump-in		
Technical rehearsal		
Musical rehearsal		
Dress rehearsal		
'OPENING NIGHT'		

7
STAGE LIGHTING

In basic terms, there are two kinds of stage lights—floods and spots. Lighting design should be completed with a strict order of priority.

1. You must first determine the *key light*—the key source of lighting for the scene (sun, lamp, fire etc.). Light the main acting areas with spotlights (e.g. centre stage, the dinner table).
2. Light supplementary acting areas with spotlights (e.g. outside window or door). In some instances, there is a good chance that steps 1 and 2) will be sufficient. If not . . .
3. Light the scenery, sets and props (e.g. backdrops, painting).
4. Flood the entire stage area to ensure that there are no unwanted darkened areas.
5. Create individual special effects from the lights which are left.

Always aim to feature the artist rather than the setting. Inexperienced lighting designers tend to start with the special effects because they are more exciting.

MAIN ACTING AREA

If you follow this very simple plan, twelve spotlights will suffice to adequately spot your main acting areas. An actor in any of the areas will be lit by two spotlights at angles of approximately 45 degrees from either side and 45 degrees from the horizontal. Without these angles the actor's face will lack shading, appearing flat and two-dimensional.

Diagram labels:
- cyclorama or painted backcloth
- three less used upstage areas (floods)
- six main acting areas (two spots each)
- Numbered positions: 7, 8, 9, 10, 11, 12 (upstage row) and 1, 2, 3, 4, 5, 6 (downstage row)

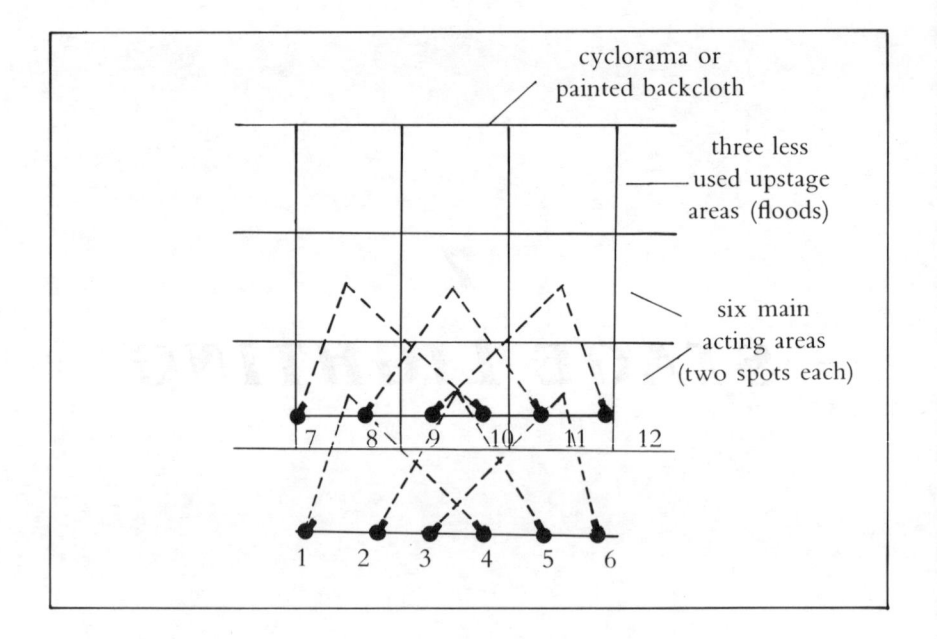

SPECIFIC LIGHTING DESIGN

INTERIOR—NATURAL

(a) All light should appear to come from windows, open doors, skylight or glass doors. Remember that you must first determine your key light—in this case, the sun (or moon, in some instances).

(b) The area and wall(s) opposite the light source should be brighter.

(c) The sun should appear to shine from one side more than another.

(d) Sunset and sunrise should be from opposite directions.

(e) Evening
- For sunset use lower angles and warmer tones.
- Shadows should appear to lengthen.
- Artificial light (lamps), candles and/or firelight to be added as the sun sets.

All changes should be undetectable.

(f) For a dull day, the overall tone should be colder and softer.

INTERIOR—ARTIFICIAL

(a) The light should seem to come from its source (lamps, etc.).

(b) The actual fittings may be used but may require masking.

Stark contrasts—lighting as an integral aspect of design. (Secrets, a Handspan Theatre production. Lighting by Philip Lethlean; directed by Ariette Taylor; designed by Nigel Triffitt.)

(c) Fittings set above head height are best because they may be simulated by normal overhead stage lighting.
(d) All fittings should be controlled by the main stage lighting board; the actor simply mimes. In this way, the source and other lights may be properly coordinated.
(e) Evening
- Aim for one main source (fire, street-light, lamp etc.).
- Use dimmer lights with cool tint.
- Specific main acting areas may be well lit, but surrounded by cool dull areas.

The power and beauty of silhouette.
(Banquet, *a Handspan Theatre production. Lighting by Philip Lethlean; directed by Andrea Lemon; designed by Trina Parker.*)

(f) Firelight

- It may be better to mask the flame.
- Several small lights are more effective than one larger one.
- The colour of fire is more yellow than red.
- Fire is seldom still but beware of intrusive scene-stealing changes.

EXTERIORS

(a) Strong shadows.
(b) Sunlight is made up of parallel beams. Therefore, focus spots and have more lamps from one particular direction.
(c) Dull days require more cool, non-directional lighting.
(d) Lighting a feature such as a wall will help to set the scene.
(e) Dawns and sunsets are more yellow/white than technicolour. Lighting should be from a lower angle for longer shadows.

(On Our Selection by George Whaley and Steele Rudd. Directed by Graeme Blundell; designed by Tony Tripp. Photo courtesy Melbourne Theatre Company.)

(The Sentimental Bloke. Photo courtesy Melbourne Theatre Company.)

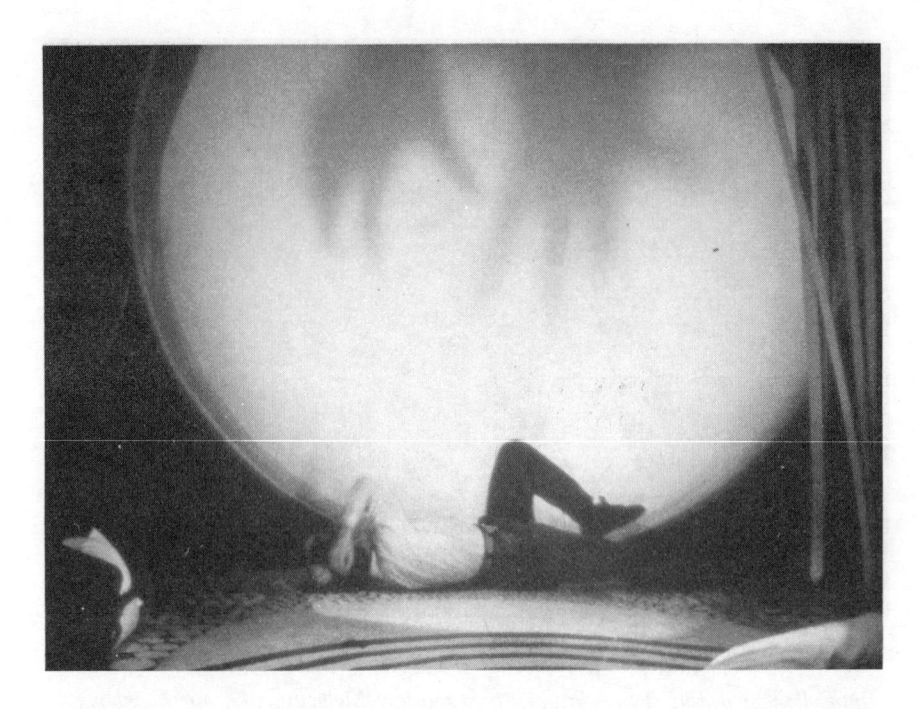

Stark, direct overhead lighting in combination with silhouette and shadow. (The Haunted, a Handspan Theatre production. Lighting by Philip Lethlean. Devised by Peter Oysten and developed by the company. Dramaturgy for the production by Helen Rickards.)

MUSICALS AND COMEDIES

(a) Remember to feature the artist rather than the setting—no matter how lavish your set may be.

(b) Although strongly artificial, a follow-spot (or two) may be effective in highlighting specific areas. They may be used with soft or hard edge, with or without filters. Two follow-spots may be set at 45 degrees.

(c) Generally, lighting should be warm and bright. If possible, save a little extra illumination for large production numbers and curtain calls.

(d) Avoid too many changes or special effects. This creates uneconomic use of available lighting.

(e) Avoid intense and cool colourings.

(f) White washes are acceptable but create a more artificial appearance than a combination of, say, subtle pinks and yellows.

*Dramatic floor lighting. (*Macbeth*, by William Shakespeare. Directed by Simon Phillips; designed by Richard Roberts. Photo courtesy Melbourne Theatre Company.)*

MOVEMENT AND DANCE

(a) Lighting must feature the dancer.
(b) Side lighting and back-lighting may be extremely effective.
(c) Artificial tones and angles are often acceptable.
(d) Lighting placed at a low angle will help to exaggerate the 'lifting' of bodies.
(e) Setting is often less important than mood.
(f) Be aware of shadows—but don't be afraid of using them.
(g) Avoid lighting that distracts from the dancer.
(h) Be aware of 'blinding' angles that create difficulty for the dancers.

THE OPEN STAGE

Some stages now have the audience on two, three and even four sides. When lighting these stages the designer must remember that lighting is required from every direction that the audience is viewing. In such instances, the lighting designer must carefully plan where each lamp will be positioned.

The stage may still be divided into nine areas, as for the proscenium stage. Four spots are required for each of the nine areas. If fewer than thirty-six spots are available, the director should determine that certain areas will be less used by the actors. For instance, four main areas may be isolated (minimum sixteen spots) by concentrating the action towards the centre of the stage. The four lights should bisect each of the four points of the square. Another method is to divide the stage into six equal squares rather than nine.

Masking is crucial when lighting the open stage. The lighting from offstage must be on a low enough angle to shine in the actor's eyes (say 35 degrees) but must not shine in the eyes of the audience. Lighting from over the stage may actually be pointed directly at the audience, so may have to be on an angle of up to 55 degrees to avoid blinding the front row. Open stages can make use of footlighting quite readily as long as masking is carefully considered.

If lighting is extremely limited, it is possible to use three instead of four lights by placing them at an angle of 120 degrees to each other rather than 90 degrees. This also applies to three-sided or thrust stages.

LIGHTING—A SUMMARY

Simplicity is the key. Your performers must first and foremost be *seen*—by all members of the audience. With a basic proscenium arch stage, start by dividing your acting area into nine equal squares/rectangles. Next, draw your set onto your grid. Determine your key light. Decide where most characters will be at most times and attempt to have each of these areas covered by two spots. Floods and fill lights are used to light the set and general areas. Spots are used to make the characters stand out from the set.

Two spots are used rather than one to try to preserve some of the natural shadows of the face and body. The basic purpose of make-up is to replace shading and contours that are washed out by the lighting. The best position for profile spots is 45 degrees on either side of the actor and 45 degrees from the horizontal. A thrust or arena stage creates further complications in that actors and sets must be lit from every audience side.

There should be an emphasis on lighting the face—especially in comedy. Musicals, light drama and comedy require brighter lighting. With limited lighting, directors and choreographers should work to specific areas. Also remember that performers should take precedence over sets and furniture.

If you have many situations where you require a single spot, a follow-spot (or preferably two) may alleviate the necessity for you to set up single spots all over your stage. They can point to wherever you need them at a particular time; it is also easy to change filters and focusing. They are not particularly suited to total realism, however. Floods usually require masking to ensure that no light spills onto the audience or onto any 'non-performing' areas.

An audience likes some variation, but remember that you are showing off the performers and not the lights. In most cases, the best lighting is that which the audience does not even notice.

Even in professional theatre, concessions are made to the limitations of lighting. Interval is generally the only time filters or focusing may be altered during a show. Beware of tying up your lights with colours or focusing that are only required for short or specific periods. If you are limited to twenty lights, it is wrong to tie half of them up with special effects or colours that will only be used for short periods.

Lit areas can also be increased by positioning the spots in wide focus or taking them further from the stage area. This will, however, reduce intensity.

Plan your focusing in advance and don't skimp on the time spent—good focus saves a lot of heartaches in the plotting stage. 'Plotting' here refers to the pointing of lights towards particular areas. Beware of 'hot spots'—areas that appear inconsistently bright because of poor focusing. Depending on your type of globe, filters may be required to counteract the cold white effect of bare bulbs.

If more than five years old, your bulbs will be incandescent, i.e. they have a filament similar to a household globe. These globes tend towards a more yellow colour and may, with minimal colour added, produce a naturalistic feel. A tungsten halogen globe, on the other hand, using the same power as an incandescent bulb, will produce two to three times the brightness. Although this saves power and creates a greater intensity, the light tends to be a cold blue colour. Colour correction may be needed to take out the blue.

Some intense and cool colours are particularly uneconomical in terms of available light. Don't forget backdrops, scenery and furniture. Avoid black areas of stage. The less you have your characters moving around and the less scenes change, the easier it will be to light.

When lighting (and painting) sets, be aware that cool colours recede and warm colours tend to move towards the eye. Any colour that you choose will have some effect on the mood of the piece you are lighting. With limited lighting, most of your choices will be based on compromise rather than the ideal.

ACTIVITIES

1 Spotlights

(a) Experiment with lighting from the front, rear, side, top and floor level. What effect does each give?

(b) Experiment with changing the focus of a spotlight. What effect does a hard or soft edge give? Try to avoid hot spots—which are very bright areas. The cast light should be of an overall consistent brightness.

2 Coloured spots

Set up two spotlights at 45 degrees to either side of an actor. Experiment with various colours in the two spots.

(a) Same colours—whites, yellows, warm and cool colours.

(b) Similar colours—whites, yellows, warms and colds.

(c) Contrasting colours—which colours make the best combinations? Will a cool and a warm colour match?

(d) Realism—see if you can find suitable colours for candlelight, moonlight, sunlight and firelight.

3 Coloured floods

Place a number of coloured floods at floor level and experiment with the colours of the shadows that are cast. Where a number of colours are used, shadows will not appear black but as combinations of the colours. Shadows also work well with backlighting and a screen. A screen can be as simple as a white sheet. Terylene curtaining material also works well. Folds can be avoided by nailing the screen at the top and bottom to a long piece of wood or dowel. This also assists with the hanging and storage of the material.

4 Floods

Try flooding a very specific space without allowing any spill. Focusing and direction are important here. If your floods are not equipped with barn doors, you can make masks for them. Be aware that many lights are too hot for plastic or cardboard to be used. Avoid moving hot lights, as bulbs are then at their most vulnerable. Simple floods can be created by masking lightbulbs. This helps to focus the beam. At all times, remember that lights are dangerous electrical items. Any metal or combustible item that comes in contact with a light is potentially lethal.

5 Overhead projectors

Experiment with the use of an overhead projector for shadow movement. Screens with rear projection may be used for shadow puppetry and to introduce scenes or give credits. Cardboard cutouts can look most effective and colours are readily available. Letraset can be used for headings. Overhead projector colours are not suitable for stage lights as they are susceptible to heat. Overhead projectors can be positioned quite close to the screen and still create a strong and large area. The shape of the area can easily be altered with cardboard cutouts.

Some ideas:

- A young couple sits in a carriage driving through a park.
- Two people meet in a red heart as the sun sets.
- Two snorklers meet. Use a flat glass bowl of water on the projector with someone blowing bubbles into it. Remember that you are using an electrical device and avoid any spillage. Flippers and snorkels can be cardboard shapes. Jaws appears.

6 Projectors

Experiment with the use of projectors to create scenes. Do not rely on flat screens. A number of lightly coloured and differently shaped blocks or screens will readily accept projections. Use two projectors to achieve a three-dimensional effect. Slides are readily available, but others can be taken as required or even photographed from pictures in books. As well as artistic or abstract scenes, try to create jungles, the bush, a city street, a desert scene or an internal scene from a public building, such as a gallery. When you have mastered this you may wish to experiment with the use of 8-mm movie film to create settings. You may project from the front onto characters or settings or as rear projection through a screen.

7 Gobos

A gobo is a shape which is projected through a spotlight. Gobos work best with spotlights which can be focused. This gives a hard edge to the gobo and allows it to be used for realism. Effects may also be achieved using lack of focus. Some floods allow limited use of gobos.

Commercially produced gobos from Roscoe.

Design your own gobo for fire, leaves, city lights, lightning, a church window and clouds. Lighting companies have catalogues of their own gobos which you can purchase or from which you can copy. Aluminium is easily cut by a stanley knife and will be suitable for many lights. Nail holes will create the effect of small lights—such as city lights. The metal you use must be resistant to quite considerable heat. If you do not know exactly where a gobo should fit, do not experiment; ask an experienced lighting technician.

Next time you visit a running creek, stream or river, look carefully at the reflections on the surface of the water.

- What colour are they?
- What patterns do they create?
- How do they move?

Invent a method of reproducing the ripple effect of water, making use of at least one gobo.

ACTIVITIES

Specific scenes

Try these lighting exercises. Don't forget to use interesting angles and shadows. Add props as required.

STAGE LIGHTING 117

(a) A sunny day turns into a cloudy, overcast sky.
(b) As the sun sets, a desk lamp becomes the main light.
(c) Dawn (lighting changes should be imperceptible).
(d) The inside of a farmhouse on a very sunny day.
(e) A cold room lit only by an open fire.
(f) A forest fire rages from miles away.
(g) An entire city in flames.
(h) Candlelight.
(i) A hospital.
(j) An actor peeps into a window at night.
(k) An actor peeps out of a window on a sunny day.
(l) A moonlit walk next to a river.
(m) A desert at midday.
(n) The cabin of a ship on the open sea.
(o) Daytime in a castle.
(p) A moonlit night on the battlements of a castle.
(q) Encores for a musical comedy.
(r) Midnight in a graveyard.
(s) A television studio.
(t) The Academy Awards.
(u) A storm.
(v) Grandma's front room.
(w) A moving train.
(x) A lift.
(y) A huge ballroom.
(z) Midnight to midday to midnight—with changes so slow that they are undetectable.

8
SOUND

Most rehearsals do not take place in the actual performing space. It is often not until the final sessions of preparation that sound is considered. Try to make it a rule to check all aspects of sound—music, voice, acoustics and technical equipment—at the earliest possible time. A quick run-through of a short scene may be all that is required to pinpoint strengths and deficiencies. These may then be considered and dealt with at subsequent rehearsals.

The dress rehearsal is not the time to discover that most of the cast cannot be heard or that the entire piece is dominated by 'background' music. In particular, remember that an empty auditorium has different sound qualities to one that is full of people.

Three aspects of sound are particularly important to consider for a theatrical production—reverberation, reflection and absorption.

Reverberation is the length of time a sound lasts. Large empty halls with reflective walls and high ceilings have extended reverberation times and, in extreme cases, echoing. Reverberation may be reduced by filling the hall with people or hanging absorbent material such as banners or carpet on the walls. In extreme cases, consider performing in winter, as everyone in the audience will be well rugged up with sound absorbing clothing.

All solid flat surfaces reflect sound to some degree. Soft surfaces tend to absorb sound. A set made of foam or canvas will absorb more sound than a solid wooden or metal set.

A curved cyclorama will reflect sound in many directions (hopefully to the audience). An angular setting is likely to have pockets where sound may be lost and areas where sound will be reflected at unusual or unexpected angles. Always consider sound when designing a set.

Directors should consider the set when blocking. Delivering a line to an open window may see the line disappear into space. The same line delivered to a foam wall is likely to be lost somewhere in the artificial bricks. Delivered to a solid surface, the line may have some chance of being reflected to the audience.

Tiered seating is not only advantageous in terms of increased visibility. Sound is also enhanced because raking reduces the 'grazing' effect—the reduction of sound levels caused by the audience absorbing some of the sound emanating from the stage. Staggering the seats, so that each person is peering between the two heads in front, not only improves visibilty, but reduces grazing. In multi-purpose auditoria, where, by necessity, the floor space for seating will be flat, it is worthwhile considering portable rostra or retractable seating to improve both visibility and sound.

Unless it is absolutely essential, avoid amplified sound. The problems inherent in mixing amplified sound often outweigh the advantages. Lessons on voice production are a far better way of overcoming quiet delivery than resorting to amplification. In many cases, you will be amplifying your problems as well as your sound. A poor singer or actor with questionable delivery or pitch will not be a better performer with the aid of a microphone.

To override the sound of a band or orchestra, some singers may feel compelled to use a microphone. The preference, however, should be to lower the volume of the music by masking, softer playing, using acoustic rather than electric instruments or moving the instruments further from the stage. Another alternative is to add a chorus of singers.

There are many sound hiring places which can offer advice but, once you leave the premises, you are often very much on your own.
Some questions:

(a) If the microphones are fixed:

- Which mikes should you choose—shotgun (single point), omnidirectional (general direction), unidirectional (single direction) or radio mike (no wiring)?
- Where are they to be hung or placed so that they pick up but do not distract?
- How do you avoid foot sounds and shuffles being picked up?
- Where will the mixer be situated?
- What path will the wires take from the mikes to the mixer?

(b) If microphones are not fixed:

- Do you require radio mikes?
- Where will the mikes be left when not in use?

- How will a character pick up and leave a mike?
- Where will the wiring be situated?

Additionally, there will be problems of speaker positioning which will influence feedback. This is a high pitched whine that occurs when the sound of a microphone goes into the speaker to be picked up again by the microphone. This process will continue to the point of deafening scream. Speakers also need to be positioned so that the sound actually seems to be coming from the characters on stage—no mean feat.

As a general rule, amplify voice only for singing—and even then, as a last resort. As well as basic projection tips there are also a number of other ways to improve sound:

- Have lines delivered directly to the audience from downstage.
- Have lighting bright enough so that faces—and mouths in particular—may be clearly seen.
- Have as little stage movement and shuffling as possible.
- Reduce speeches to one or two sentences by sharing them between characters or rewriting them.
- Make projection a principal criterion for casting.
- Consider sound when choosing the theatre space.

If you happen to be stuck performing in a large hall or gym, it may be better to perform on the floor with the audience around you than to stay on stage. Wooden floors can be extremely noisy and it is worth considering putting old carpeting, material or even cardboard on the floor in the aisles or under the seats. Oiling seats and doors may reduce extraneous noise.

Large halls will echo in open spaces, so it is worth sealing off unused sections with material, banners, streamers, cardboard or anything that will help muffle the sound. Walls, especially brick, will bounce the sound around and carpets or curtains hung on them will help considerably. A parachute or material hung from the roof will not only be decorative but will reduce annoying echo and keep the sound in the vicinity of the audience.

The traditional proscenium stage is fraught with danger in that sound delivered to the wings tends to disappear there. Sound delivered from upstage has difficulty clearing the curtaining that often surrounds the stage.

Be aware that your audience will absorb a percentage of your sound. A full house wearing thick woollen coats in winter will absorb more sound that a few skinny kids in shorts. It is important to bump up your sound levels during rehearsal to compensate for this loss of sound. It is a good idea to make the actors aware of this.

Better projection is not yelling. Most of the rules of projection are common sense; posture, breathing, relaxation. If you have no training or are unsure, there are many good books on the subject. Voices should not be allowed to strain during the rehearsal period. Larger character roles, especially during the later rehearsals, should be carefully monitored and, when appropriate, rested. It is a good idea to have specific 'quiet' rehearsals.

The ear will adapt to the noise level that it encounters. An audience may be able to hear much of a very quiet show that is persistently quiet. They will learn to listen. If however, the quiet dialogue is interspersed with loud pop songs, then do not be surprised if the dialogue begins to pale by comparison. If you have a quiet show, the most suitable opening music would be at an almost inaudible level—prompting the audience to listen carefully.

That being said, and for all my insistence on not using a sound system, if your audience cannot hear your show, you have no show. Don't wait for the dress rehearsal to consider sound. Start from the first audition and rehearsal, and from the first moment you view your theatre.

ACTIVITIES

1 The group divides into two lines who face each other from the furthest extremes of the studio or theatre. Each group member has a partner in the opposite group. Each individual is given or invents a message which must be passed to their partner in the opposite group. The difficulty, of course, is that everyone will be delivering their message at the same time. Avoid straining, be clear and repeat as slowly and as often as possible. After each delivery, both partners may take one step forward.

2 Two actors move to opposite extremes of the studio or theatre. Their task is to hold an intimate conversation which is loud and clear enough for both to hear, but which maintains a sense of intimacy.

   Try:

   (a) a marriage proposal
   (b) a romantic supper
   (c) a secret
   (d) a confession
   (e) an embarrassing visit to the doctors
   (f) a favour
   (g) planning a crime
   (h) a phone call
   (i) bad news.

III
IN CONTEXT

9
COMEDY

ORIGINS

The Greeks invented theatrical comedy in Athens in the fifth century BC. Aristophanes (448–380 BC), with works such as the *Wasps, Birds* and *Frogs*, was the chief exponent of Old Comedy—a style which demanded a strict and formal interplay between actors and chorus. After a transition through Middle Comedy, which had less emphasis on chorus and more on plot, New Comedy was born.

New Comedy was a far cry from the staid classical Greek model which made use of a formal chorus. Menander, the best known of the New Comedy poets, used a chorus who had very little to do with the plot—often arriving as a group of singing drunks. Stock characters were used for the first time—a convention later taken up by Roman comedy and later still by the commedia dell'arte. New Comedy also introduced the convention of an actor speaking on stage, unheard by a second actor. We still accept this convention today.

From 240 BC, with the first translation of a Greek drama, the Romans built on and extended classical Greek conventions. Terence (190–159 BC) introduced a 'persona' or character created through mask, later adapted by the commedia. Taking his art seriously, he used few jokes, buffooning or comic moments not integral to the plot.

Plautus (approx. 254–184 BC) may have lacked the subtlety of Terence, but he made up for it with the stock-in-trade of great comedy, vitality and wit. His works provided the basis of Shakespeare's *Comedy of Errors* and even, in 1962, the American musical, *A Funny Thing Happened on the Way to the Forum*. Plautus also introduced the convention of a prologue.

In time, the Romans, especially the lower classes, tired of Terence, Plautus and the classical Greeks and turned to pantomine. It would be many years before these influences would combine to create the theatre of the commedia dell'arte. Greece was the birthplace and Italy the cradle of modern comedy.

With the banning of plays in Italy in 1548 (England followed suit in 1588), something very silly was bound to happen. That something was the development in the sixteenth century of a style of theatre that combined the conventions of the Greeks and Romans. It was an entirely improvised style of comedy, making use of masks and stock characters and situations.

These endearing characters have endured today. Harlequin, the jester, the pomp deflater, the individual who questions authority with laughter; the ultimate clown to whom so many clowns owe so much—including many silent films stars. Pulcinella, he of the large nose and hunch back; appealing ugliness, the loveable rogue—a mass of contradictions; adapted through European culture in puppet form as Punch. Pedrolino or Pierro, playing with powdered face and without mask—the traditional white-face clown we have come to know as Pierrot.

Puppeteer Greg Temple with old friends Punch and Judy.

The basis of an endless line of mime artists such as Jean-Gaspard Deburau, Etienne Decroux, Jean-Louis Barrault and eventually Bip, the alter-ego of Marcel Marceau—one of many clowns to join the Pierro family tree.

There is not a single comedy, or for that matter, piece of theatre which does not owe something to the comedy stock types of the commedia dell'arte. By the end of the seventeenth century the commedia dell'arte was in decline, but not before its influence had spread far and wide. Clowns and fools were a staple of Elizabethan theatre. The farces of Lope de Vega (1562–1635), regarded as the founder of Spanish theatre, owed much to the Italian commedia troupes.

In France during this period a golden comic age was dawning through the works of Racine (1639–99) and Molière (1622–73), and the performances of the Comédie Française, which was officially founded in 1680. In a perfect blend, the French brought together the best influences of the Greek, Roman and commedia traditions. Molière's 'Comedy of Manners' found its natural evolution in the eighteenth century in the works of Sheridan, in the nineteenth in the works of Oscar Wilde and perhaps even Chekhov, and in the twentieth century in the works of Noel Coward.

The Comédie Française today. Here performing Moliére's Le Bourgeois Gentilhomme *at the 1988 Melbourne Spoleto Festival—now known as the Melbourne International Festival of the Arts. (Photo courtesy the Victorian Arts Centre.)*

To this day, the Comédie Française acts as a stabiliser of tradition; preserving and passing on the repertoire and style of the past.

Back in England during the late-seventeenth century, Restoration Comedy was about to raise its bawdy head. Through the works of such writers as Congreve and Farquhar, the world was shown to be a place inhabited by opportunists and fortune hunters; often ruled by the stupid but controlled by the street-wise. It was a world of inverted moral values. It signalled the entry of women on the English stage for the first time, although they had been an integral part of French and Italian theatre from the earliest times.

There were to be no more golden ages of comedy, with comedy becoming, as it remains today, merely one of many tools in the hands of the playwright.

Every comedy owes something to the past. No sketch or style that exists today could be said to be wholly original. New formats are invented and new material written, but the comic flowers of today are grown from the seeds of comedy's distant past.

COMIC STYLE

SATIRE

The Greek poet was required to present a burlesque of three tragedies (often, not always, a trilogy) and one 'satyre' play. In this, a hero from myth (often from the tragedies) was placed in ludicrous situations. It was the precursor to the concept of comedy relief—a convention whereby an audience is given 'time-out' for a laugh during a harrowing tragedy. Today, 'satire' is the name given to a 'send-up' or exaggerated scene which lampoons and often mocks its subject.

PANTOMIME

Pantomimus, a Roman dancer, has given his name to this art of many meanings. Pantomime was initially the label given in Imperial Rome to an actor who created a character from mask and gesture alone. It was later used to suggest all acting without words—mime being a shortening of the term. Its current use is generally confined to the Christmas Panto—up until recently an eagerly anticipated part of the Australian theatrical calendar. With roles such as 'Principal Boy' and 'Dame', and with variety acts interspersed with fairy-tale action, the pantomime was, for many years, traditional Australian Christmas fare.

The first all-Australian pantomime was *The Bunyip*, which opened at the Grand Opera House in Sydney in 1916. It saw Roy Rene cast as Mo Lazarus, J. C. Williamson as an understudy and Queenie Paul—

a perennial of Australian variety (she opened her last show in 1980)—as Principal Boy.

SLAPSTICK

It has come to mean physical or knock-about humour. The origins of the term derive from the stick used by Pulcinella in the commedia and later by Punch, and from the stick carried by the Court Jester. In later clowning, an actual slap-stick was used. Today, no stick is required, though a prop such as a ladder is often crucial to a slapstick routine. This playing round is often known as 'business' or a 'bit'.

FARCE

Historically, farce refers to scenes of buffooning which were inserted into early religious dramas. In modern times, it is generally regarded as a piece with great entertainment value and little literary merit. Farce is based on improbable situations with the protagonist at odds with the environment. It was popular in the eighteenth and nineteenth centuries in England and America in one-act plays. Feydeau (1862–1921), the French dramatist, is the most celebrated writer of farce. Regarded in his day as a purveyor of light entertainment, he has since received just recognition as a writer of classic farce through the restaging of his works by the Comédie Français.

BURLESQUE

In commedia, a burla (plural 'burle') was a comic interlude usually involving a practical joke. The term 'burlesque' initially referred to a satire such as *The Beggars' Opera* (1728) which parodied both opera and drama. In modern terms, a burlesque generally refers to the American risque shows which proliferated in the late-nineteenth century. A training ground of stand-up, Al Jolsen, Sophie Tucker and W. C. Fields all made a start in burlesque—as did Gypsy Rose Lee, whose claim to fame was not comedy. A type of pantomime for adults, burlesque found its way to Australia and was eventually edged off the stage here by comic opera and musical comedy—family rather than filthy entertainments.

VAUDEVILLE

Vaudeville is burlesque for the family. Originally a satirical song based on a popular tune, it has come to refer to all kinds of performances consisting of a number of novelty, music and comic acts. Referring to England, we would tend to use the term 'music hall' and referring to America, 'vaudeville'. Today, we tend to use the term 'revue' to describe a disparate collection of performances.

MUSIC HALL

Flourishing in the second half of the nineteenth century in England, music hall was the logical development from the pub sing-along. Eating, drinking and specialty acts were orchestrated by the chairman, who guaranteed a good time was had by all. Australian music hall started in Melbourne in the 1850s in response to demands for entertainment during the Gold Rush. It initially suffered from poor housing and audiences more disposed to drinking than aspects of the programming.

In 1890, Harry Rickards established the first permanent music hall in Australia in Castlereagh Street, Sydney. As The Garrick, it suggested links with jolly old England; renamed the Tivoli, it became part of Australian theatrical history. Rickards eventually operated Tivoli's in Sydney, Melbourne and Adelaide. Fuller Brothers, from New Zealand, went one step further and established a complete Australian circuit. Three of the great talents of Australian comedy, Jim Gerald, George Wallace and the legendary Roy Rene (Mo) all worked the Fullers Circuit.

Mo, king of Australian comedy, is regarded by many as a comic genius in the company of Chaplin. Although Fullers' motto was 'Hilarity without Vulgarity', it was generally regarded that any dirty joke doing the rounds could be attributed to a sketch from Stiffy and Mo—Stiffy being Roy Rene's comic foil, Nat Phillips. A master of the double entendre, Mo's classic response was, 'Blue? I'm not blue. It's all in their dirty filthy minds.' A black-and-white caricature of a Jewish Australian with a lisp, Mo had as many incongruities and contradictions as Punch.

CONTEMPORARY AUSTRALIAN COMEDY—A MELBOURNE PERSPECTIVE

Melbourne has played a leading role in the development of Australian comedy and theatre generally. It is one of the few places in the world that would claim an almost unbroken line of development from the early days of music hall to present day theatre restaurants. In the early sixties, while most of the rest of Australia found the concept of a theatre restaurant to be a little tawdry and passé, Melbourne's 'Tikki and John's' was boasting that it was booked out two years in advance.

Roy Rene—alias Mo McCackie.

Theatre restaurants are now an integral part of the comic theatrical landscape of every Australian state.

The character of Edna Everage (now Dame Edna) first appeared on the stage of the Union Theatre, Melbourne, in a revue entitled *Return Fare* on 13 December 1955. It was a two-hander, as distinct from the monologues we have grown used to. Noel Ferrier and Gordon Chater both variously played the second role. Ray Lawler, the Union Theatre

Repertory Company's resident writer/director and another actor, Peter Batey, are credited with suggesting the part to Humphries as an extension of one of his party characters. Dame Edna lives on.

The Union Theatre Repertory Company developed into the Melbourne Theatre Company. It claimed actors of the calibre of Fred Parslow, Zoe Calwell, Frank Thring, and George Fairfax, one of the driving forces behind the establishment of the Victorian Arts Centre—not bad for a struggling university drama group. One of its first directors was John Sumner, who continued with the MTC for another thirty years before retiring in 1989. Sue Nattrass, current General Manager of the Victorian Arts Centre, was a stage hand before going on to join 'The Firm', J. C. Williamson's, the home of Australian musical comedy.

The late-fifties at Melbourne University saw the biggest breakthrough in Australia's short theatrical history. Ray Lawler's *Summer of the Seventeenth Doll* stunned Australian audiences before taking on London. This production proved that Australian theatre had an identity entirely separate from its British and European heritage. For the first time, we were not importing ideas and productions; we were exporting.

Thirty years after The Doll, in 1987, Simon Palomares combined with Nick Giannopoulos and school teacher, Maria Portesi, to devise *Wogs Out of Work*. Initially, the show was a Fringe offering for Melbourne's own Comedy Festival. *Wogs Out of Work* has introduced an entirely new audience to the theatre. It has been no less revolutionary or influential as *Summer of the Seventeenth Doll* was in its day. Approaching half a million paying customers, WOW has broken the record for attendance for an Australian written piece—long held by The Doll. Time will determine its lasting importance.

Comedy in particular and theatre in general received some of its strongest impetus from the fringe theatres of the sixties. The Australian Performing Group worked from a Pram Factory in Carlton. Much of Carlton's current life and appeal is directly attributable to the fringe theatres which made it a place to be and be seen.

Writers of the calibre and stature of David Williamson, Jack Hibberd, Alex Buzo and John Romeril honed their skills on shows that were a direct reflection of the social circumstances of the times. Actors such as Max Gillies, Graeme Blundell, Evelyn Krape, Jane Clifton, Tony Taylor, Lindy Davies and Bruce Spence learned their craft with the APG.

Many of the performances and performers have not lasted in theatre, but their contribution to the theatre that we know today remains significant. Circus Oz, Captain Matchbox and Playbox Theatre directly or indirectly owe their existence to the APG.

The Hills Family Show, Back to Bourke Street, Stork, Don's Party, Chicago Chicago and *Dimboola* are not much performed today. In their

Edna Everage pre-Dame—about 1956.

Zoe Calwell in Blithe Spirit—*1953.*

time they were at the forefront of a theatrical revolution that swept Australia; a revolution that cleared the collective psyche of the all-pervading European traditions and prepared us for the endemic Antipodean contemporary theatre, especially comedy, that was to develop in future years.

By the late-sixties, the cultural cringe in Australian theatre was more likely to be the name of a new coffee lounge than a legitimate negative force.

Theatre led and film followed. Some of the best works, actors and directors found themselves, on film and stage, contributing to the great search for Australian identity; a search led, appropriately enough by comedy. The disruptions of the sixties meant something different for every country. For Australia, it was a search for what being Australian meant. With television primarily made up of British and American fare, Australians found their identity at the theatre.

The comedy of the future will be, as it has always been, both a comment on and a reflection of the age. If you want to know what kind of age we live in, what quality of life we enjoy, in what direction

Summer of the Seventeenth Doll *opens in London in 1957, directed by John Sumner.*

The Doll—then . . . (Melbourne Theatre Company, early sixties.)

The Doll—. . . and now. (Australian Nouveau Theatre, late eighties. Directed by Jean Pierre Mignon; designed by Wendy Black. Photo by Jeff Busby.)

Wogs out of Work—*original cast, writers and co-producers: Nick Giannopoulos, Maria Portesi and Simon Palomares. (Photo courtesy Hocking and Woods.)*

The Hills Family Show *at the Pram Factory. Evelyn Krape in a wheelchair and the audience behind.*

we are heading, look closely at the comedy that surrounds you. It is more than just a way to make you laugh—it's a sign of the times.

ACTIVITIES

1. (a) Choose three jokes, three joke tellers and three audiences.
   (b) Choose three time periods by which joke tellers will pause before giving the punchlines (say one second, two seconds and three seconds).
   (c) Work out a system to determine how funny jokes are—a laughometer.
   (d) Decide:
      (i) who told the jokes the funniest (delivery)
      (ii) which jokes were the best (material)
      (iii) which timing was the most successful.

2. Find out about stand-up comedians and their styles.
   (a) Which of them tell supposed 'true' stories?
   (b) Which of them play characters other than themselves?

3. Write your own monologue.
   A monologue is a series of stories which are linked to make sense. They are not jokes, as such, but the stories generally contain humorous incidents and characters. Sometimes one story is interrupted by a number of others. The classic story commences, 'A funny thing happened to me on the way to the theatre . . .'

4. *Straight/funny*
   Where two or more comedians work together, one of the two generally assumes the role of straight (adult/normal/sensible) person. The other is generally stupid, clumsy or prone to unusual, unexpected or incongruous actions and statements. This combination of the child-like naive one and the sensible one has been a constant as long as there have been comedy teams. Stiffy and Mo were the classic Australian team, with Stiffy being generally 'straighter' than Mo. Los Trios Ringbarkus broke from this mould when they determined to be as incompetent as each other.
   Who is the straight person in these comedy teams?
   (a) Abbott and Costello
   (b) Laurel and Hardy
   (c) Dean Martin and Jerry Lewis.
      Which other Australian comedy teams have worked in this style?

5. *Slapstick*
   Comedians throughout the ages have made use of clubs (Punch)

and props to hit, bash and cudgel. This has been refined into a stick used in music hall, vaudeville and clowning known as the slapstick.

(a) Which comedians do you know who use mainly slapstick to get their laughs?

(b) Why do we laugh when something slapstick happens to a character—say, falling over or a paint pot falling on someone's head?

(c) Would you laugh more at a rich businessman being covered in paint or a painter? Why?

(d) Devise a silent slapstick sketch with two builders attempting to erect the wall of a house.

6 *Embarrassment*

(a) Why do we laugh at sex, bad language, toilet humour and embarrassment?

(b) What is the most embarrassing thing that ever happened to you? Was it funny?

7 A *sketch* or blackout is a short humourous scene.

(a) What are common subjects for sketches?

(b) What makes a topic suitable for a sketch?

8 *Satire* is another name for 'send-up' (taking the mickey, lampooning, exaggerating).

(a) What is satire?

(b) What makes satire funny?

(c) In what ways may a 'normal' scene be made into satire?

(d) Write a satire about your family or friends.

9 A *situation comedy* generally depends for its humour on a domestic humorous situation.

(a) Make a list of television's current situation comedies, taking note of exactly what the humour is based on.

(b) Are there differences between British, American and Australian styles of humour?

(c) Which are recorded live and which use laugh tracks?

(d) On average, how many jokes are told per half-hour?

(e) Choose one situation comedy and make a list of the subject matter of the humour. Look for jokes and humour based on:
- character flaws
- quirky behaviour
- stupidity

- unlikely situations
- misunderstanding
- cute children
- the generation gap.

How much of the humour is based on character as compared to situation?

10
DRAMA

ORIGINS

Drama has followed its own tortured, meandering, though inevitable path. Sometimes it travelled with comedy, at others it wandered aimlessly on a solitary path. I leave its discovery to you. From the earliest drama of the Greeks, discover what you can of the origins of drama as we know it today.

The history of comedy was virtually complete with the development of the commedia dell'arte. Few revolutionary movements of significance have altered the basic commedia formula. Today, on stage and screen, we still watch characters and situations which owe their existence to the commedia.

In contrast, many significant drama movements have occurred in contemporary rather than ancient theatres. In drama, it often seems more relevant to discuss the latest revolutionary trend than to delve into the historical perspective. For this reason, I have chosen to concentrate on some of the important contemporary movements in drama and leave you to pursue your own exploration of history.

To accomplish this successfully, choose a particular perspective, such as:

- influence of the church
- women in theatre
- the use of masks
- social and political influences
- influences on a particular writer and how this writer then influenced others.

Choose one area of particular interest and collate the results of your group for a broader perspective.

CONTEMPORARY MOVEMENTS IN DRAMA

AVANT-GARDE

The avant-garde was a movement influencing all of the arts in the latter part of the last century. The movement was in reaction to the staidness which had preceded it. One of its chief exponents in theatre was Alfred Jarry, through his play *Ubu Roi*—an unabashed parody of Sophocles' *Oedipus Rex*. Its elements of coarse unsophistication and crude theatricalities shocked the audience of its day. Its first live presentation was in 1896. In the twenties, the avant-garde extended its influence into surrealism and dada. The absurdist movement, especially the work of Jean Genet, had its roots in the avant-garde.

NATURALISM/REALISM/ EXPRESSIONISM

Realism began with Hendrik Ibsen in the nineteenth century as a reaction to the artificiality of the stand-and-deliver style of drama which was then in vogue. Ibsen set normal characters in domestic situations and gave them natural speech. Naturalism, through such writers as August Strindberg, took the process a step further by attempting to banish all artificiality to produce theatre both stark and confronting. Both writers made use of the box set, a room cut away on one side and designed to offer a 'slice of life'.

Expressionism, later influenced by dada and surrealism, began in Germany in 1910. It was to have a profound effect on Brecht, who embraced many of its principles. It was a reaction against the complacency of naturalism, realism and, in art, impressionism. It replaced their staid and safe view of life with enthusiastic idealism and a questioning of values. The later works of Ibsen and Strindberg contributed to the expressionist movement.

DADA/SURREALISM

Dada was founded in Zurich in 1916 and was a strong artistic movement of the early twenties. It depended for its effect on shock, outrage, and the incongruous and unexpected. It is most closely associated with surrealism, another movement of the twenties, which was an attempt to explore pure thought without the intervention of reason. Neither movement, as much by definition as any other factor, has created lasting important works of theatre. Their influence on other theatrical movements, however, has been profound.

ALIENATION

Alienation was one of the principal effects employed by Bertolt Brecht with his Berliner Ensemble, which he formed in 1949. Brecht had been experimenting with alienation and his concept of epic theatre since 1922. The basis of alienation is that the actor and audience be allowed to stand aside from the character being portrayed to allow a semblance of objectivity. Alienation refers not only to acting style but any effect or mechanism designed to reduce the subjectivity of presentation. Brecht explored his theories of alienation and epic theatre through his own plays and direction. His work and theories have profoundly influenced contemporary theatre.

METHOD

Method is a style used by many of today's actors. It is a logical method of study devised by Constantin Stanislavsky, based on simplicity and truth. A rejection of the false declamatory style of acting of his predecessors, 'method' is based on empathy with and personal understanding of a character. It contrasts with Brecht's theories of objective alienation. Any contemporary actor pursuing a role must

Stanislavsky's production of Gorky's The Lower Depths, *Moscow Art Theatre. (Courtesy of the Theatre Collection, New York Public Library.)*

balance the subjective approach of Stanislavsky and the more objective style of Brecht.

THEATRE OF CRUELTY

In the early part of the century, Antonin Artaud conceived of a theatre which would take language from its central theatrical pedestal and replace it with symbolic gesture and sound. Artaud hoped to unconsciously disturb theatregoers and force them to see themselves as they really are. Artaud saw the theatre as a catalyst of action and change. His theories had a profound influence on the writings of Jean Genet and the work of English director Peter Brook, himself a strong influence in contemporary theatre.

THEATRE OF THE ABSURD

This term, coined by Martin Esslin, describes the work of a number of playwrights of the fifties and early-sixties; it includes Samuel Beckett, Eugene Ionesco, Jean Genet and Harold Pinter. In their world, the irrationality and incongruity of life are allowed to dominate reality. Their works seek to discover a greater theatrical reality by overturning what we generally regard as real. There is a suggestion that life is basically without meaning and communication is in a state of total breakdown. This leads to an emphasis on pause and silence. Many regard its finest work as Beckett's *Waiting for Godot*. As a pure form, the absurd had had its day by the early sixties, but its influence remains a vital force in contemporary theatre. Even comic writers such as Tom Stoppard are not untouched by it.

POOR THEATRE

Jerzy Grotowski set up his experimental Laboratory Theatre in Poland in 1959. Its work has been a major influence on European and American contemporary drama. Grotowski believes that the actor is at the core of the theatrical art. All other theatrical trappings are regarded as peripheral in this pure theatre—or 'poor' theatre. Grotowski's influence has reached Australia indirectly through the tours of Peter Brook, an advocate of pure, or poor, theatre.

INTERNATIONAL CENTRE FOR THEATRE RESEARCH

In 1970, Peter Brook created this Centre in a disused tapestry factory in Paris. Brook had come to international prominence in that year with his production of *A Midsummer Night's Dream*, which toured a number of countries, including Australia. Directed by Brook for the Royal Shakespeare Company, the production breathed a special life into Shakespeare, which helped to rejuvenate a contemporary thirst for classics. Without changing a single word, Brook produced a contemporary piece from a classic text.

Brook's International Centre for Theatre Research brought actors from around the globe to experiment with and search for a common theatrical language, free of the constraints of common speech. It is a search which was begun by Artaud. The work of the Centre has been prodigious and highly acclaimed. *The Conference of the Birds*, Jarry's *Ubu Roi* and the Indian marathon epic, *The Mahabharata* all toured Australia and left an indelible mark on the Australian theatrical landscape.

A quarry in the Adelaide hills provided a unique setting for Brook's The Mahabharata *and* The Conference of the Birds. The Mahabharata. *A play by Jean-Claude Carriere based on an epic Sanskrit poem. Adapted into English and directed by Peter Brook. Designed by Chloe Obolensky. Brook's Paris-based company included thirty-two actors and musicians from twenty-three countries. It was a co-venture involving the Royal Shakespeare Company, Brooklyn Academy of Music, Los Angeles Festival, City of Zurich, Australian Bicentennial Authority and Adelaide Festival. (Photograph by Philip Martin, courtesy of Adelaide Festival Centre.)*

THEATRE CONVENTIONS

The first Greek plays took place, with a chorus of fifty, in an amphitheatre sculpted out of a hillside. They were later to take place in a make-shift theatre known as a 'theatron' or 'seeing place'. By the age dominated by New Comedy, the third century BC, the importance and number of the chorus had diminished and the actor had to be 'presented'. This led to the convention of the raised stage.

The Romans invented mass concrete and were able to construct elaborate theatres in every one of their city states. Their stages were divided from the auditorium by a large curtain, the first use of such a device.

After the fall of Rome in AD 476, theatre continued on its tortured path through the ages, with one convention replacing another—liturgical plays performed in churches with elaborate scenery and stage mechanics; commedia dell'arte often performed from the back of a cart; theatre performed in opera houses and backstreets.

No convention existed in isolation—influencing not only other conventions of the period but also those that were to follow. Theatre conventions are the essence of theatre history. They are a direct reflection of the times.

ACTIVITIES

Through research, what can you discover about the historical conventions of the following?

Theatres

- amphitheatres
- the raised stage
- curtaining
- open air performance.

Staging

- raked stages
- open stages
- theatre-in-the-round
- the fourth wall.

Scenery
- box sets
- scenic painting
- flats
- flies.

Lighting
- sunlight
- footlights
- candelabra and candles
- gas
- limelight.

What are the historical conventions related to the following?
- directing, producing and managing
- acting
- props
- costumes
- make-up
- stage machinery.

Choose one area of particular interest and collate the results of your group for a broader perspective.

11
THEATRE—THE UNTOLD STORY

There are many theatre histories—each with its individual perspective; floral tributes to the past ornamented with petals of changing shape and hue. The following is an historical perspective that serious scholars have tended to overlook—sordid anecdotes and juicy tit-bits; subjective analysis neither all-encompassing nor seriously scholarly, but perversely fascinating, all the same.

AUDIENCE—WHY ARE WE HERE?

'The cinema has thawed out people's brains.'
—*Jean Cocteau*, 'Opium', 1930

Michael Green, in his book, *The Art of Coarse Acting* refers to an audience of schoolchildren as, 'simply a collection of malevolent minds waiting for an excuse to make a noise'. Nicol Williamson became so incensed by audience noise during a schools' performance of *Macbeth* at Stratford in 1984 that he stopped the show. He threatened to restart the play and to continue to do so each and every time there was further disruption. The performance continued in silence.

Television has destroyed much of our concept of quiet absorption. It is not unusual for someone today to be watching television, listening to the radio, reading the paper, doing homework and carrying on a conversation—all at the same time. Television is offered to us in ten-minute slabs broken by sometimes hideous and intrusive tattle known as advertisements. People walk in front of and away from the television at regular intervals. Conversations must be held over the noise of the television. At dinnertime, the television continues—sometimes unwatched, sometimes in the kitchen accompanied by the sounds of mastication and digestion.

Is it any wonder, when ten minutes is the normally required attention span, that ninety-minute films and three-hour live theatre productions have some difficulties in maintaining complete audience attention? A film will survive the odd heckler and whisperer; many live productions will not. Once, the audience was raised on theatre; films and television arrived as a novelty. Now the novelty is live theatre and audience protocol simply is not being learned as it used to be. We hear complaints of lateness and talking, lack of response and failure of appreciation. The following offers some insights into audiences of an earlier age. It should provide much food for thought for those who bemoan the loss of the genteel and totally absorbed theatregoer and pine for a return to the glory days of bygone eras.

The first London theatres were seldom noted as places to absorb culture. In a letter written by the Lord Mayor and Alderman of London to the Privy Council in 1597, four basic objections to the theatre were raised. The objections were that theatres corrupted youth, attracted vagrants, maintained idleness and spread germs (because sick people tended to frequent them on their days off). Other writers were even more forthcoming in their attacks. Henry Crosse wrote in 1603 that an audience was made up of:

> ... for the most part the lewdest persons in the land, apt for pilfery, perjury, forgery or any rogueries; the very scum, rascality, and baggage of the people, thieves, cut purses, shifters ... an unclean generation and spawn of vipers ... For a play is like a sink in a town, wherunto all the filth doth run; or a boil on the body, that draweth all the ill humours into it.[1]

Unkind perhaps but, reportedly, accurate. Elizabethan theatregoers were indisputably a spirited and involved audience. Complaints such as, '... the spectators frequently mounting the stage and making a more bloody catastrophe amongst themselves than the players', were commonly reported.

The early French theatre seems to have been even more dangerous. In 1640, François Hedelin wrote of the companies of 'debauchees' coming in and, 'committing a hundred insolencies, frighting the Women and often killing those who take their protection.'

Samuel Pepys noted in 1663 that the reputation of theatre was so poor that ladies often wore a mask (visard) to the theatre; either for reasons of anonymity or to ensure embarrassed blushes remained unseen. Queen Anne forbade their use in 1704.

The problems were made doubly difficult because of the custom of having spectators on stage with the actors. There were complaints of

Snug in the Gallery: *Theodore Lane's depiction of a boisterous audience in the eighteenth century.*

ladies sitting with their backs to the players and spectators involving themselves in the action. Take this reference to when Garrick portrayed Lear in Dublin in 1762:

> When the old King was recovering from his delirium, and sleeping with his head on Cordelia's lap, a gentleman stepped at that instant from behind the scenes, upon the stage, and threw his arms around Mrs Woffington, who acted that character . . .[2]

Or this, from Garrick's *Romeo and Juliet*:

> What a play it must have been whenever Romeo was breaking open the tomb of the Capulets, with at least two hundred persons behind her, which was to convey the idea of where the heads of all her buried ancestors were packed.[3]

Or this, from Holland's *Hamlet*, dating from about the same period:

Masked Venetians at the Box Office. Engraving by de Pian. For Act III, Scene xii of Goldoni's La putta onorata *in Opere teatrali, Zatta edition, Venice, 1791. (Yale Theatrical Prints Collection.)*

> On seeing the ghost he was much frightened, and his hat flew off his head. An inoffensive woman hearing Hamlet complain the air bit shrewdly, and was very cold, with infinite composure crossed the stage, took up the hat and with the greatest care placed it fast on Hamlet's head.[4]

While the English and French were thus enjoying themselves—what were the Venetians up to? Venice . . . ah, home of culture. Let us peep into a theatre in 1678 and watch the nobility in action:

> The young Nobility do not go so much to the Comedy to laugh at the Buffoonry of the Actors, as to play their own ridiculous Parts. One of their most ordinary Diversions is not only to spit in the Pit, but likewise to pelt them with Snuffs and ends of Candles, and if they perceive any one decently clad, or with a Feather in his Hat, they are sure to ply him with the best of their endeavours.[5]

Imagine what the common folk were up to!

On 23 April 1759, spectators were banned from the stage of the Comédie Française, and David Garrick followed suit for Drury Lane in 1763.

Spectators on the English stage. Hogarth's painting of a scene from Act III ('When my hero in court appears') of Gay's The Beggar's Opera. *(Photo by R. B. Fleming & Co., London.)*

In France, in 1782, the custom of the standing pit ceased and Mercier wrote that, 'No sooner was the audience made to sit down during performances, than it fell into lethargy.' A situation, some would claim, that continues today.

New York had its first theatrical season in 1750 and, after some initial Quaker opposition, things got off to a rollicking start. By 1802, culture had crossed the Atlantic and the Americans were really getting into the swing of things—just like their English cousins. This report is from Washington Irving:

> The noise in this part of the house is somewhat similar to that which prevailed in Noah's ark; for we have an imitation of the whistles and yells of every kind of animal. Somehow or another, the anger of the gods seemed to be aroused all of a sudden, and they commenced a discharge of apples, nuts and gingerbread, on the heads of the honest folk in the pit. A stray thunderbolt happened to light on the head of a little sharp-faced Frenchman, who seemed to be an irritable little animal. Monsieur was terribly exasperated; he jumped upon his seat, shook his fist at the gallery, and swore violently in bad English. This was all nuts to his merry persecutors; their attention was wholly turned on him, and he formed their target for the rest of the evening.[6]

In 1845, the American actor, Forrest, visited England and was hissed as Macbeth. Assuming that his rival, Macready, was responsible for this hostile reception, Forrest reciprocated when Macready played Hamlet in Edinburgh. This led to the bloody Astor Place riot on 10 May 1849, when Forrest's American partisans clashed with Macready's admirers. Hundreds took to the streets and the National Guard and New York police were called out in full force to quell the disturbance.

J. M. Singe's *The Playboy of the Western World* met a rowdy reception (in fact, near riots) on its opening night at the Abbey Theatre, Dublin, in 1907. Joseph Holloway recorded in his diary that an 'unusually brutal coarse remark . . . set the house off a-hooting and a-hissing . . till the curtain closed in. Two days later, after a 'terrific uproar', the manager came on stage to castigate the offenders, 'You who have hissed tonight will go away saying that you have heard the play, but you haven't.' 'We heard it on Saturday!' came the reply and the uproar began anew.[7] Nineteen years later, Sean O'Casey's *The Plough and the Stars* brought similar riotous reactions: 'While part of the audience stormed the stage to attack the cast, another section waged war on the rioters themselves.'

The Astor Place Riot (1849)
From an engraving in The Illustrated London News, *June 2, 1849. (Courtesy of the Theatre Collection, New York Public Library.)*

Theatre at its best!

These, of course, are only the historical 'highlights' of colourful audience response. Many a performance has naturally been completed in silence and with more refined audience reactions than attacking the cast or 'frighting the Women'. They do show, however, how vulnerable the theatre and the performer are to the whims of the audience.

The very first European theatrical production on Australian soil was performed by convicts in June 1789. A group of convicts at Botany Bay asked Governor Phillip if they could produce a play in honour of the King's birthday, and he agreed. The play was Farquhar's *The Recruiting Officer*. Tiberlake Wertenbaker's *Our Country's Good*, a recent play on the Australian scene, describes the hectic lead-up to the historic production. Thomas Keneally's *The Playmaker* is based on the same theme. As there were no reports of escapes during the presentation, it must be assumed that the audience were on their best behaviour.

In terms of the first Australian theatrical event, *The Recruiting Officer* was predated by 40 000 years. The plays of Jack Davis are European in structure, but they are a logical progression of the storytelling and understanding of life through art that has always characterised Aboriginal culture.

The Recruiting Officer by George Farquhar.
(Directed by Kim Durban; designed by Tony Tripp. Photo courtesy Melbourne Theatre Company.)

In a culture which lacks the written word, theatre and storytelling become the cornerstones for the passing of knowledge and history from one generation to the next. The dancer/actor/storyteller is not only entertaining his audience, he is providing the building blocks from which the wisdom of the next generation will be built. Stories told are more than mere fancy, they explain the very basis and reason for the existence of life itself. Is it any wonder that a full house and total concentration are guaranteed? Theatre becomes natural, ordered and flowing—an integral part of being.

Each generation has much to learn from the past. Theatre is the manifestation of the storytelling that is basic to the human species.

There are some works, such as Shakespeare and farce, which maintain an almost universal acceptance whenever they are staged. Others must accept the whims of a collective psyche which is dependent on artistic taste and divided along national, socio-economic and, in Australia, even state boundaries. Some works and productions are lauded proudly and others given an unkind raspberry.

To have the key to any particular audience psyche, to know exactly what will please and displease them, would prove more fruitful than borrowing Midas' right hand. To directors, performers and playwrights, it must sometimes seem near-impossible to determine what will work from one audience to the next.

The second of two identical performances may suffer simply because it is identical. It may lack that magical and invisible spark of originality and immediacy that made the first performance so memorable. It may simply be that the second audience was smaller, quieter or less inclined to be kind—providing only stifled interplay between audience and performer. This is the true fickleness of theatre and what makes it so exasperatingly unpredictable and thrilling.

In the short term, television does not particularly care what its audience thinks—or even if it thinks. It affects the performances not one iota. Theatre audiences have an immediate and all-pervasive control of proceedings. Their reactions are stepping stones to the scenes that are to follow. Every nuance of a performance is dependent for its vivacity on previous and immediate audience response.

Philosophers and existentialists may disagree, but let us be clear—without an audience there is no theatre. Films and television may continue to run long after the holocaust has rendered their audience with less than unceasing interest; not so, theatre.

Just before their untimely and tragic deaths, both Judy Garland and Tony Hancock were booed by Australian audiences. Some performers seem to be extremely dependent on this fickle, nameless and forever-changing mass we know as audience. Theatre thrives under its good graces but withers under its scorn, derision or indifference. The quality of the theatre we experience in the future may very well depend on the quality of audience that it attracts.

ACTING – THE SECOND OLDEST PROFESSION

> "In the theatre the audience want to be surprised—but by things that they expect."
> —Tristan Bernard (1866–1947), Contes, Rèpliques et Bon Mots.

Nowadays actors are regarded with the greatest awe—they have sex appeal, are hero-worshipped, courted by the socially conscious and are offered accolades and peerages. Few in society may hold their head higher than a successful actor. It was not always so. The history of theatre is cratered with actors of greater and lesser renown—fabulous successes and abject failures.

The earliest recorded theatrical record dates from 534 BC. Solon, a legislator, visits Thespis (you've heard of thespians?) in his dressing room after a performance and asks, 'if he were not ashamed to tell so many lies before such a number of people?'[8] Inadvertently, Solon had become the first theatre critic—and actors had started to develop a poor reputation. Solon, of course, had missed the whole point, which still remains a prerequisite for being a critic today.

The Elizabethan era is generally regarded as a cultural age. Ships set sail for the New World. The boundaries of Empire were expanding with the consciousness of the populace. Elizabethan music was developing in a refined, petite and delicate manner. The cobwebs of the Dark Ages were being swept away and preparations were well under way for European renaissance, reformation and revolution. They had much to sweep away.

Back in the fourth and fifth centuries AD, the Christian Church had taken an extremely dim view of theatrical types. One decree from a Church Council read: 'It shall not be lawful for any woman who is in full communion . . . to marry or entertain any Comedians or Actors; whoever takes this liberty shall be excommunicated.'[9]

Strong stuff indeed! Unfortunately, little had changed by the enlightened Elizabethan age. One of the laws of the land read: 'All Bearwards, Common Players of Interludes, Counterfeit Egyptians, etc. shall be taken, adjudged and deemed Rogues, Vagabonds and Beggars and shall sustain all pain and punishment.'[10]

It took a long time for women to appear on the English stage. This did not occur until the court of Charles II during Restoration times, the sixteenth century. The Puritans, just as the Christians before them, objected to it strongly as it might introduce debauchery to the theatre—as, of course, it did.

Tom Brown, the seventeenth century satirist, had this to say:

> It is as hard a matter for a pretty woman to keep herself honest in the theatre, as 'tis for an apothecary to keep his treacle from the flies in hot weather, for every libertine in the audience will be buzzing about her honey-pot.[11]

This did not, however, stop many a talented lady from trying her hand at acting and perhaps even attracted a few. The three most influential female actors of the early English stage were Hannah Pritchard (1711–68), Peg Woffington (1714–60) and Sarah Kemble Siddons (1755–1831).

It was said of Hannah Pritchard that, 'Her distinguishing qualities were natural expression, unembarrassed deportment, propriety of action and an appropriateness of delivery.'—a far cry from Tom Brown's 'honey-pot'.

She was one of the first to give female roles the prominence they deserved—the equal to, if not better than, their male counterparts. It must be remembered that men had been playing both the male and female roles since before Shakespeare's time. It was a fitting tribute that when she played Lady Macbeth for the last time, in 1768, her long-time partner, David Garrick, vowed that he would never play Macbeth again.

Sarah Siddons is regarded as the greatest ever female player of tragedy. One contemporary critic wrote that she was 'tragedy personified'. After she retired, it was written, 'Who shall make tragedy stand once more with its feet upon the earth and its head above the stars, weeping tears of blood?'

Peg Woffington had a harsh voice which, apparently, made her unfit for tragedy. Turning this to her advantage, she determined to turn the tables and play both male and female roles with deft execution and gusto. She achieved fame and respect playing 'breeches parts'—the convention whereby a female dressed as a male and played a male role. This convention was, by the way, one of the formative elements of the 'Principal Boy' in pantomime.

There have been many great actors on the stage, but few have created the impact of Charles Macklin (1697?–1797), John Kemble (1757–1823) or David Garrick (1717–79)—the first of theatre's male acting giants. Each had a distinct style which contributed to the development of acting as we know it today.

Charles Macklin, in 1773, broke convention and played Macbeth for the first time in historical costume. Previously Macbeth had been dressed as a contemporary officer. Lady Macbeth, for this production, was still dressed in the height of contemporary fashion. Macklin was also the first, in 1741, to play Shylock as a dramatic rather than a comedy role. A change obviously long overdue.

John Kemble continued the revolutionary trend in 1794, where he

Charles Macklin as Shylock. Engraving. (Courtesy of the Theatre Collection, New York Public Library.)

started to clean up the 'little things' such as the witches in Macbeth wearing, 'mittens, plaited caps, laced aprons, red stomachers and ruffs'.[12] This was a dress convention handed down from David Garrick's Macbeth. Or little things like a Roman centurion standing in front of a backdrop of a Surrey countryside and walking into a chamber, 'the walls of which were ornamented with pictures of various events in the history of England'.[13] By 1794, people had started to notice these 'little' discrepancies.

Just as Thespis has given his name to all actors, the name Garrick conjures up images of all things theatrical—acting, actor/managers and theatres. The terms 'Garrick' and 'theatre' are inseparable. Garrick is the most famous and most respected of all of the early actors. Garrick's style was described as 'easy and familiar—yet forcible'. It was a style which threw critics into some hesitation regarding the propriety of his approach. By today's standards he would surely be regarded as a more formal player. Here is how one contemporary critic described his Hamlet encountering the ghost:

> ... (Garrick) staggers back two or three paces with his knees giving way under him, his hat falls to the ground and both his arms, especially the left,

Garrick as Hamlet. Engraving. (London, Victoria and Albert Museum.)

are stretched nearly to their full length, with the hands as high as the head
. . . his mouth is open . . . thus he stands rooted to the spot, with legs apart
. . . supported by his friends.[14]

Although Garrick could strike terror with such a pose, many of the contemporaries who attempted to follow suit merely looked ridiculous. In its time his style was regarded as revolutionary and rivetting. His influence on his contemporaries was profound.

By 1805, stage technique had become so poor that Thomas Holcroft was compelled to compile a list of ills in his *Theatrical Recorder*. The entrenched habits listed by Holcroft included performers looking about them and gesticulating to known audience members, reading personal correspondence in stage, leaving through the wrong door or where there was no apparent apperture at all, starting every sentence with a gesture from the right hand and continuing to alternate with every sentence, stepping forwards and backwards with each alternate sentence, shaking a finger or hand for the entire duration of a speech and (shades of Garrick) standing with the arms horizontally in front for speechmaking. Technique was lacking, and learning lines heightened the problems.

During an initial halcyon period in the early days of theatre, actors were not bound to 'study more than eighty-four lines of tragedy or one hundred and sixty-eight of comedy within twenty hours'. But by 1852 it was not infrequent to see actors expected to learn from three to five hundred lines during the day for an evening performance. As the saying goes, 'there was many a slip . . .' Actors tried many methods of approach. Edmund Tearle was famous for his novel method of overcoming 'drying'.

> If he failed to master his words he would quite literally go on and make a noise, stunning the audience with a series of bull-like roars and gentle bleats, from which not one single word was intelligible.'[15]

The concept, of course, was to deliver these noises with such assurance that the audience would be fooled. It would be up to the other actors to keep the audience up to date with plot and content. On such occasions, some fellow actors resorted to running their lines together into one long speech—thereby saving time and embarrassment.

We, perhaps, should not be too critical. It was common for players to receive only a copy of their own lines—with pertinent cues included. Exacerbating this lack of detail, leading players were loath to rehearse more than necessary and flatly refused to exhibit any form of emotion for the entire duration of the rehearsal period. Some leading players carried blocking and costumes with them from production to production regardless of set or context. It was not uncommon for players to have absolutely no idea what happened in any part of the performance except for the ones in which they were particularly involved. Opening nights were truly a wonder to behold.

Some are great, some have greatness thrust upon them and some are just plain awful.

The worst actor ever is generally regarded as Robert 'Romeo' Coates. A number of factors made him immensely popular, including his habit of wearing diamonds from head to foot, regardless of the role, his tendency to 'improve' on Shakespeare as he went and his practice of laying a white handkerchief on stage for a death scene. One critic wrote of his Romeo in 1807:

> . . . the play got as far as the last act, but ended in riot when Coates suddenly entered with a crowbar, which was quite unnecessary and not mentioned in Shakespeare's text, to prise open the Capulets' tomb.[16]

His Lothario in 1811 was, apparently, an even greater triumph:

> ... Coates took longer to die on stage than anyone before or since. The audience sat politely, as his writhing figure was gripped by spasm after spasm.[17]

But he wasn't finished. After interval, he cancelled the next act and, instead, recited his favourite monologue. You simply can't keep a good man down.

Few actors are now regarded as rogues or vagabonds—that title being reserved more often for unscrupulous theatrical management. It has been an extremely arduous and hazardous journey on the road to respectability. Villified and persecuted, maligned and shunned—no other profession lays itself so open to criticism on every working day.

After such a colourful history, who could now begrudge actors a few of life's little luxuries—like being President of the United States?

Actors are the litmus of their age. They absorb from and illuminate the world around them. They are a distorted mirror into which we peer; the reflection of all that we could be. They show us our true selves by stripping away parts of our own being. They are the projectors of myth and the ultimate reality. They are the artists who use their own bodies as canvas and you and me as paint. We peer at them but, in reality, we are in their zoo; a glass menagerie of broken fragile humans.

A true actor is an artist who creates, not from a vacuum, but from the reality that surrounds. The act of creation is not one of pulling rabbits from hats or plucking cards from thin air. The true creative artist, the true creative actor, creates by taking your world apart and reordering the pieces into another reality.

We need actors. They are the window into our inner selves. We treat them like travelling salespersons—we should treat them like gods.

ACTIVITY

Choose a topic of historical theatrical interest to you and, through research, find out all you can about it. Collate your group's efforts into a mini-history of theatre. Some possible areas of research are listed below:

- television viewing habits
- French theatre
- early American theatre
- Macready
- early Australian theatre

THEATRE—THE UNTOLD STORY

- Jack Davis
- audiences in other cultures
- Thespis
- Roman theatre
- women in theatre
- Hannah Pritchard
- Peg Woffington
- David Kemble
- theatre managers
- theatre in non-Western cultures
- sixteenth century England
- Drury Lane
- Forrest
- Irish theatre
- Aboriginal culture
- contemporary audiences
- Greek theatre
- Elizabethan theatre
- the Restoration
- Sarah Siddons
- Charles Macklin
- David Garrick
- other styles and periods

NOTES

All of the numbered quotes in this chapter are from two sources:
A Source Book in Theatrical History by A. M. Nagler, Dover, 1952 [referred to in the notes below as *Source*]; and
The Book of Theatre Quotes by Gordon Snell, Angus and Robertson, 1982 [referred to in the notes below as *Quotes*]

1 *Quotes*, p. 21
2 *Source*, p. 381
3 *Source*, p. 382
4 *Source*, p. 380
5 *Source*, p. 526
6 *Source*, p. 526
7 *Quotes*, p. 1
8 *Source*, p. 3
9 *Quotes*, p. 51
10 *Quotes*, p. 4
11 *Quotes*, p. 5
12 *Source*, p. 413
13 *Source*, p. 413
14 *Source*, p. 368
15 *Quotes*, p. 10
16 *Quotes*, p. 65
17 *Quotes*, p. 65

12
STAGE VERSUS SCREEN

There can be little doubt that television is a medium that has affected each of us profoundly. It is inextricably bound up with every major occurrence. It weaves into our dreams; it translates our fears; it offers visual evidence of what is happening throughout the globe by way of daily satellite pictures from space itself.

It came as no surprise when researchers found that many children spent more time in front of the box than in the classroom. The young of today are the first to have grown up with television from their earliest moments of consciousness. If they were lucky, they may have even relived their own birth on dad's VHS, which he just happened to take with him to the hospital.

We are rearing generations of voyeurs—those who may gratify their every whim by merely tuning in. No areas of our universe are ignored—we can travel to the stars or search for meaning in the reproductive processes of an amoeba. All are subject to the probe of the television camera lens. Television governs our moods, fills our time, determines our tastes. Unlike God or Big Brother, it may not be all-powerful and all-knowing, but there can be little dispute that it is ever-present. Conversations revolve around it and games are played on it.

Children do not worship television but, like disciples, they avoid questioning their viewing habits. They may not sing hymns praising it, but it is the exceptional child who does not know by heart a multitude of signature tunes and advertising jingles. Some of these same children have difficulty remembering that 'two two's are four'. If nowhere else, the rote system has worked for television.

We are living in the future. Most people now learn more about the world from satellite pictures than from travel—and this is a trend which will continue. As telecommunications increase their influence across the globe, the need to travel diminishes. Why walk when you can phone? Why go to the world when the world can be delivered to your doorstep? As computers and television intertwine, their combined force will sever even further our links to a past life based on the experiential rather than the voyeuristic.

Shopping may now be completed via the television. The last links with our primal hunter–gatherer past are being swept away in an information boom that will revolutionise humanity. The challenge of the future is to fully appreciate the fact that the future is already here. The problem is, we don't realise it—we're too busy watching television!

On television, I have watched sweat work its way through a sweat gland. I have followed food down a gullet. I have watched computer graphics blur the line between what is and is not—turning reality into a kind of malleable clay rather than absolute stone.

I have counted the hairs of a spider's legs and watched, through a lens, the rings of Saturn and the moons of Jupiter and Neptune. I have travelled through the tail of Halley's Comet and viewed galaxies far, far, away. I have seen the bluish hue of neutrons, the building blocks of the universe, in a nuclear pile.

How can theatre compete with the magic of reality—whether cosmic or microscopic? Easily. Reality?—you can keep it! The magic of theatre is the magic of the imagination freeing the soul from the constraints of everyday existence.

Theatre was born in an ancient Greek amphitheatre two thousand years ago. Aeschylus, Socrates and Euripides unlocked a formula that has persisted to this day. They did not find the building blocks of life—they discovered the key to existence itself—a method of exploring the meaning of life. Their concerns were not with the nuts and bolts of life, nor even with the engine—they were more concerned with the very purpose of the journey.

The theatre is no accident. It is humankind's response to the vagaries of the gods—eternity, existence, life after death. Theatre seldom strives to show us urine flowing through a urethra but it may, as Aristotle attempted to explain, offer us a catharsis—a cleansing—through the theatrical experience.

Theatre allows us to wallow in the world of another so that we may be cleansed of the stultifying existence in which we are trapped. For a short time, we are given the wings of the gods to look on humanity from above; to see with all-seeing eyes—to be given what no person may achieve in reality; the benefit of hindsight, the foresight to know what is yet to be. As audience, we become Dionysus—God of Theatre, of excess, of euphoria, of having a good time.

Television and film also offer visions, but they lack immediacy. The best films are repeated, unchanging, for audience after audience. They neither know nor care who is watching. There is no dialogue between audience and film.

It is sobering to contemplate the fact that the laughs, guffaws, hee-haws and chuckles on many American sit-com laugh tracks were recorded in the fifties. The chuckles may belong to individuals who are long since deceased, or who are currently dying of some painful terminal illness. Think on that when next you join them for a chuckle.

Most television and film happened in the past in a time frame far, far away. They are not played out before us—here and now. Television is like life continually played and replayed through a slow-motion camera or video; look at that; review that; analyse that bit; let's go back to the start; seen this before—who cares; ads, yuk, zap!

It has to be better to be at the game than to watch the winning kick replayed in slow motion. Otherwise, why do anything at all?

Theatre is for those who want to experience events. No two performances are identical—each performance depending for its existence on a dialogue between actor and audience. Television and film provide the safety of the predictable, the expected, the unchangeable. Film is larger than life; television is life cut into bite-sized pieces; and theatre is life itself.

Theatre exists as a series of immediate moments—no single moment interchangeable with another. It happens. Like a conjuror's trick, there is little point in reading the book, looking at the photo, watching the film, replaying the event or hearing about it later. Like the funny joke—you just had to be there.

'You know what happens?
People go to the movies instead of moving.'

Tennessee Williams, The Glass Menagerie

ACTIVITY

Divide your average day, week, month and year into an hourly breakup of time spent on the following activities:

(a) watching television

(b) being in a classroom

(c) going to the pictures

(d) sleeping

(e) going to the theatre

(f) eating

(g) relaxing

(h) partying
(i) writing
(j) playing sport
(k) working
(l) other.

How many hours are spent 'doing' as compared to 'viewing'?

1 What do the results tell you about yourself?
2 What trends are apparent in the group?
3 How would the results compare to those of, say ten, fifty or one hundred years ago?
4 What trends are suggested for the future?
5 If we spend more time on an activity, does this suggest that it is necessarily better or more enjoyable? What other factors influence how we choose to spend our time?
6 Are there any differences between the results of boys and girls?

13
CRITICISM

'The object of art is to give life a shape.'

—Jean Anouilh

THE SEARCH FOR MEANING

Humankind has always had an insatiable desire for creativity and self-expression. All cultures possess at least some basic semblance of music, drama and dance. It is with some disbelief that we continue to hear knowledgeable scientists proclaiming that Stone Age man drew on the walls of caves solely to assist with the hunt. Did drawing have to be so practical?

It is not beyond belief to suggest that people of the Stone Age gained no lesser satisfaction from creativity—the production and appreciation of—than we, ourselves, experience.

Aboriginal culture is as ancient as any left in existence. Aboriginals may not have built the pyramids or put in a freeway bypass around Ayers Rock, but their concept and appreciation of art is as developed as any other race or culture on earth. In art, we are all equals; no one better or worse; some merely more knowledgeable, practised, skilled or spontaneous.

We are born with art, a gift from our forebears. We are touched in exactly the same way that humankind has always been touched by art—through a combination of head and heart. When you feel strange rumblings and note a glow of warm recognition, you are participating in an experience that began with the first human being and has been shared by every human since. Tastes and cultures vary, but art, music, drama and dance are eternal and universal.

THE CRITIC AS ARTIST

One of the great difficulties of art for young people is understanding the layers of ideas and techniques that combine to produce the finished product. It is simply not good enough to react to art with, 'I know what I like'.

Two colours on a canvas divided by a straight line may not appear immediately to the viewer as exceptional art. When we learn that the artist has spent a lifetime exploring the relationships between colours, then the exact position of the divisional line takes on added significance.

The demand for realism in art, which many young people claim to 'like', really is the search for a myth. The Mona Lisa is not realistic. It is a two-dimensional rectangle of strangely coloured oil paints, which is not even lifesize. Our eyes allow for these differences and our absorbed impression is that of something real. Reality then, is what we choose to see as real.

The Egyptians chose to draw reality in profile only; Picasso chose to represent some faces in profile and from the front at the same time; Walt Disney chose to draw Mickey Mouse always with both ears facing frontwards—no matter which way Mickey was facing. We allow for these changes to reality because we 'know what they mean'. A significant proportion of visual art is produced in two dimensions and black and white. The boundaries of realism are in a continual state of flux.

Theatre is not reality. It is a carefully designed series of guidelines and signposts which we, for maximum appreciation, must learn to decipher and interpret. The theatre box set is not a room with one side cut away—it merely represents one. Blue light is not night light, and yet we accept it as such without question.

Art may be judged on more grounds than simply whether it is pretty, realistic, or tells a simple story. To fully appreciate what an artist means by a piece, we must try to follow the artist's processes. Instead of simply asking, 'Do I like that?', we have a whole new range of questions to ask.

'Why did the artist choose this topic?'
'Why did the artist choose to work in this style?'
'What is the artist trying to say?'
'Which of the artist's aims were fulfilled and which not?'

These are questions which help the viewer to stand in the shoes of the artist. This allows us to follow through the process of creation rather than standing outside the piece and handing out our judgments in ignorance. The more we do this, the more we become the artist. We work through a piece, take it apart, look at each piece and put it back together again—just as the artist has done.

Some young people find it difficult to understand that it is not the role of art to reach out and grab them—it is the role of the audience to enter the world of the artist and search out what the artist has to offer. To do this, they must know how to be an artist. The totally passive critic, waiting for something magical to simply happen, may be waiting a very long time.

Performance art is no less of an art form than drawing, painting or sculpture. Art may generally be defined as more than the sum of its constituent parts. Red, green and blue lines may come together to create more than a series of meaningless colourful lines. In the hands of an artist, three lines may move us profoundly, tell us something about ourselves or, to extend the argument, offer the meaning of life.

In theatre, the constituent parts (lighting, sound, acting, design, direction and backstage) must come together to create a product which is much more than the sum total of its individual processes. It is important for us to be able to unravel (or deconstruct) theatre to identify and explore its constituent parts. It is equally vital to understand how to piece individual processes together to produce great theatre. This is the role of the true artist/critic.

ON THE ATTACK

There are multitudinous elements that combine to create a poor production. Rather than continually attack the actor, a critic should carefully and separately consider all of the elements that contributed to the production. It is seldom that everything will be right or wrong with any particular production.

The fact that a director and designer have made inappropriate choices and dressed everyone as vegetables, is no reason to assume that the efforts of the actors and technical crew should be overlooked. True, it would be difficult to fully appreciate *Hamlet* with the cast dressed as vegetables. The fact remains that this is a director's and designer's mistake rather than an actor's or technician's. A critic's opinion should be coloured, not completely distorted, by such decisions.

An actor may choose an affectation which is totally offensive or grating to the critic—say, a deep cough or scratching of the private parts. This is a single choice amongst many that combine to create the character. This character, other characters and the production itself are not total disasters because one character has made one inappropriate choice.

Critics should avoid attacking a production for what it is not and what it never intended being. A production of *Hamlet* with the actors dressed as vegetables should not be judged as if it were a poor version of the Royal Shakespeare Company. It is apparent that such a production would not purport to be anything even remotely resembling the RSC.

The production may have failed to achieve Shakespeare's intentions, but the director may have had individual intentions which were admirably met. Judge a piece on its own intentions.

A critic should deconstruct a performance, but the role of critic does not then involve reconstructing the piece in another form. 'What would I have done in the circumstances?' is a common enough response. The answer to this question should not be allowed to dominate what is, after all, a response to the work of others.

TERMINOLOGY

In writing about or discussing any piece of theatre, it is essential to be precise. We are living in an age of 'mini-speak'. Positive and negative comments are confined to 'good' or 'grouse' and 'bad' or 'boring'. Fewer words are remaining in common usage. The less a word is used correctly, the more it sounds inappropriate and pretentious when used correctly.

In theatre, 'wonderful', 'marvellous' and 'fabulous' have replaced, for many, the need for more expressive adjectives. They are gushed around with little care or thought as to exactly what they may mean. Describing an opening night as 'wonderful' has virtually come to mean no more than that the curtain actually went up.

A quick run-down of the exact meaning of some common descriptions reveals:

wonderful	exceeding what was expected
marvellous	extravagantly improbable
fantastic	rare or eccentric
fabulous	given to legend
dreadful	full of dread or fear
awful	worthy of respect or fear
revolting	full of loathing or disgust
terrible	exciting terror
appalling	prone to make one lose heart; become dismayed

In describing or offering opinion about theatre, we must attempt to make use of exact terminology which differentiates between varying degrees of success and appreciation. We must go deeper than the single overriding impression left by the production. We must ask ourselves what moments of joy, boredom, excitement, wonder and frustration were fused at the moment the lights came up for the last time. The critic must go beyond general impressions, and the general terminology that accompanies them, and search for the heart of a piece—the elements that made it tick.

> ## ACTIVITY
>
> Is 'revolting' worse than 'appalling'? Make a list of twenty words commonly used to describe productions. Place the words in order from most to least approving. How much agreement is there among members of your group?

DECONSTRUCTING A PLAY

PERSONAL RESPONSE

- Was I stimulated, provoked, inspired, outraged, angered, entertained, disturbed, upset, distressed, amused, bored or frustrated?
- Did I enjoy the experience?
- Did I learn something?
- Did I feel that it had something to say?
- What did I feel after the performance—in the short and long term?
- What were the best and worst aspects of the production?
- What was the audience response?
- Would I recommend it to others?

THE PLAYWRIGHT AND PLAY

The message and intention

- What was the intention of the playwright and did the playwright succeed in this intention?
- Did the play have a message and was it clear, muddled, or hidden?
- What questions were asked and what answers offered?
- Was the piece comic or dramatic?
- Was the piece designed to teach (didactic) or entertain?

The plot

- How were plot and subplot organised?

- Was there a major theme or series of themes?
- Did the narrative unfold in a continuous or episodic fashion?
- Were there unexpected twists in the plot?
- What was the mood of the piece?
- Was the ending or plot predictable?
- Was the plot interesting?
- Was there a climax or anti-climax or series of them?
- Did the playwright make use of symbolism (one thing standing in place of another)?

The language

- Was the language formal or colloquial, poetic or naturalistic, period or contemporary, Australian or otherwise?
- Was the use of language economic or superfluous?
- Was the language appropriate?

THE DIRECTOR

- Did the director achieve the playwright's aims?
- Were the director's choices obvious?
- Did the director put a strong individual stamp on the production?
- Was all of the blocking appropriate—was it natural; was anyone masked (hidden); did the blocking reinforce the text?
- Were the cast organised as a strong ensemble (team) or did individualism predominate?
- How were all of the basic theatrical components (lighting, sound, acting, design and backstage) combined?
- Did the director have something to say in addition to the message of the play and playwright?
- How unique was this production of the play?
- How disciplined were the cast?
- How clearly did the actors understand and portray the director's intentions?
- Was it appropriately paced?
- Were the energy levels appropriate?
- What was the dynamic (ebb and flow, highs and lows) of the production?

THE ACTORS

- Were all characters clearly delineated?
- Did each actor have a clear understanding of the intentions of the play and the director?
- Were characters natural or exaggerated, realistic or stereotypes, studied or spontaneous, shallow or complex?
- Did characters show evidence of research or consideration of fine detail?
- How strong was your empathy (understanding, liking, feeling) with particular characters—how strongly did you care for or about them and what was happening to them?
- Was there a protagonist (hero) and antagonist ('baddie' or foil to hero)?
- Were mannerisms and gestures appropriate and expressive?
- Were voices clear and expressive?
- Were movements and stances natural or artificial, relaxed or uncomfortable?
- Did all actors make a strong offering to the audience and to other actors?

THE DESIGNER

- Did the designer achieve the play's intention?
- Were the designs appropriate?
- Was the overall design integrated or intrusive?
- Was there evidence of successful designer–director collaboration?
- How practical were the sets and costumes?
- Were the designs natural or artificial, realistic or abstract, overstated or subtle?
- Did the designs portray a similar message to the rest of the production?
- Did they display a creative flair?
- Did they enhance or handicap the production?
- Was the theatre an appropriate venue?

TECHNICAL

Lighting and sound

- Could everything be clearly seen and heard?

- Were lighting and sound appropriate?
- Were lighting and sound integrated or intrusive?
- Was there evidence of creative decision-making?
- Was there evidence of successful designer-director-technical collaboration?

Scene changes

- Were they smooth and logical?
- Was time used economically and efficiently?
- Were there too many changes?
- Were changes appropriate or too complex?
- How disciplined were the mechanists (theatre technicians responsible for moving scenery)?

In the final analysis, a play is presented for enjoyment rather than criticism. A spontaneous response to a production is as valid as a considered or studied opinion. The deconstruction of a play should occur only after the event.

Read the play beforehand, by all means, but you should not approach a play with your mind full of critical questions and considerations. There will be plenty of time for that later, when the curtain is down and the piece is nothing more than a lasting memory. Taking the play apart then will help you to understand this memory and appreciate the reasons behind your spontaneous responses. Your opinion can not be wrong, but it may be shallow and ill-informed. Knowing you liked or disliked something is not enough—you should know why.

THE LONELINESS OF THE LONG DISTANCE CRITIC

The fact must be faced, the professional critic is, by general consensus, far from popular. How could a true artist, a creator, agree that the toil of months, perhaps years, is mere 'bumph'; the greatest production ever a mere carbuncle on the backside of theatre?

Artists are as children blowing up balloons at a party. Critics are as dull bullies sticking pins in the balloons that appear not to be the correct shape or colour, or are not to their liking. They care little that it takes as long to blow up a 'yukky' purple balloon as a beautiful yellow one. Much has been said and written of the professional critic. Here is but a mere sample:

'Writing about art is like dancing about architecture.'

—*Anon*

'A drama critic is a person who surprises the playwright by informing him what he meant.'

Wilson Mizner

'No degree of dullness can safeguard a work against the determination of critics to find it fascinating.'

—*Harold Rosenberg,* Discovering the Present, 1973

'Asking a working writer what he feels about critics is like asking a lamp-post what it feels about dogs,'

—*John Osborne (attrib.)*

'They search for ages for the wrong word which, to give them credit, they eventually find.'

—*Peter Ustinov, 'On Critics', BBC Radio, 1952*

'Critics? They're all shining wits.'

—*Rev. W. A. Spooner (attrib.), Warden of New College, Oxford*

'A critic is a bunch of biases held loosely together by a sense of taste.'

—*Witney Balliet,* Dinosaurs in the Morning, 1962

'Criticism is not just a question of taste, but of whose taste.'

—*James Grand, 1980*

'. . . drooling, drivelling, doleful, depressing, dropsical drips.'

—*Sir Thomas Beecham, 1962*

'Critics are eunuchs in a harem: they know how it's done, they've seen it done every day, but they're unable to do it themselves.'

—*Brendan Behan (attrib.)*

'Critics can't even make music by rubbing their back legs together.'

—*Mel Brooks, quoted in the* New York Times, 1975

'. . . inkstained wretches.'

—*Alexander Woollcott*

'Mediocrity weighing mediocrity in the balance, and incompetence applauding its own brother . . .'

—*Oscar Wilde,* The Critic as Artist

THE CRITIC AS EUNUCH

. . . and why are critics such a maligned species? Here is a collection of some of the lines that have helped to place the critic somewhere on the popularity scale between Attila the Hun and a McDonald's Fillet O' Fish.

We stare at car accidents and peer with macabre fascination at disasters of all kind. Enjoy the following in a similar vein.

'Richard Briers last night played Hamlet like a demented typewriter.'
—W. A. Darlington, reviewing Hamlet, Daily Telegraph

'He directed rehearsals with all the airy deftness of a rheumatic deacon producing Macbeth for a church social.'
—Noel Coward, on producer J. R. Crawford (attrib.)

'As swashbuckling Cyrano, Mr Woodward's performance buckles more often than it swashes.'
—Kenneth Hurren, reviewing Cyrano de Bergerac, 1970

'. . . and John Mills wanders around the stage at the St James theatre looking like a bewildered carrot.'
—Review of his 1953 performance in The Uninvited Guest

'Dennis Quilley played the role with all the charm and animation of the leg of a billiard table.'
—Bernard Levin, reviewing High Spirit (a musical version of Coward's Blithe Spirit)

'Farley Granger played Mr Darcy with the flexibility of a telegraph pole.'
—Brook Atkinson, reviewing a musical version of Pride and Prejudice in the fifties on Broadway

'Mozart, played by Simon Callow as a goonish cross between a chimp and a donkey . . .'
—Bendict Nightingale, reviewing the 1979 stage production of Amadeus

'Annette Crosbie played Viola like a shetland pony.'
—Review of Twelfth Night

'Mr Geilgud has the most meaningless legs imaginable.'
—Ivor Brown, reviewing Gielgud's Romeo

'Geraldine McEwan, powdered white like a clownish, whey-faced doll, simpered, whined and groaned to such effect as the Queen that Edward's homosexuality became both understandable and forgivable.'
—Milton Shulman, reviewing Brecht's Edward II

'She has the sort of stage presence which jams lavatories.'
—Fleet Street critic Nina Myskow on actress Charlotte Cornwell (later awarded $21 000 damages for libel plus $63 000 costs)

The New York Times' George S. Kaufman was not noted for the kindness of his criticism. A press agent once asked him, 'How do I get our leading lady's name in your newspaper?' Kaufman's reply? 'Shoot her!'[1]

Others of his gems include:

'There was laughter at the back of the theatre, leading to the belief that someone was telling jokes back there.'[2]

'I saw the play at a disadvantage, the curtain was up.'[3]

'I was underwhelmed.'[4]

'A show like this could give pornography a bad name.'
—*Critic of* Oh Calcutta!

'Ouch.'
—*Full review of the Broadway show* Wham

'The producer himself gave us an effective ghost, which would be even better if he'd discard the modern craze for crediting Hamlet's father with sepulchral asthma.'
—*Donald Wolfit on Ken Tynan (later to turn critic) in the Oxford University Players' production of* Hamlet

'The Covent Garden Company is execrable. Young is the best among them and is a ranting coxcombical tasteless Actor—a Disgust, a Nausea—and yet the very best after Kean.'
—*John Keats, writing to his sister in 1819*[5]

'She was a vulgar idiot. She never read any part of the play, except her own part . . .'[6]
—*Dr Samuel Johnson, on actress Mrs Pritchard as Lady Macbeth*

'Bernard Miles played himself like an effigy of Charles Dickens attacked by a fit of the mange.'
—*Alan Brien reviewing Ibsen's* John Gabriel Borkman *in the* Sunday Telegraph

'. . . any fan of Walt Disney comics could see that he had modelled his appearance on Scrooge McDuck.'
—*Clive James writing in the* Observer *on Olivier's Shylock*

Critics and audience alike still talk of Peter O'Toole's unusual portrayal of Macbeth for the Prospect Theatre Company in 1980.

'He (O'Toole) delivers every line with a monotonous tenor bark as if addressing an audience of deaf eskimos . . .'
—*Michael Billington*, The Guardian

'He walks around the stage as if he were inspecting a property he has just acquired.'
—*Irving Wardle*, The Times

'His performance suggests that he is taking some kind of personal revenge on the play.'
—*Robert Cushman*, The Observer

Here are some choice cuts from Dorothy Parker.

'Go to the Martin Beck Theater and watch Katherine Hepburn run the gamut of emotions from A to B.'

—*Reviewing* The Lake, 1933

'. . . she had the temerity to wear as truly a horrible gown as I have ever seen on the American stage . . .
Had she not luckily been strangled by a member of the cast while disporting this garment, I should have fought my way to the stage and done her in myself.'

—*Reviewing* The Silent Witness, New Yorker, 1931

'. . . now you've got me right down to it, the only thing I didn't like about *The Barrets of Wimpole Street* was the play.'

—The New Yorker, 1931

It isn't what you might call sunny. I went into the Plymouth Theater a comparatively young woman, and I staggered out of it three hours later, twenty years older, haggard and broken with suffering.'

—*Reviewing Tolstoy's* Redemption, Vanity Fair, 1918

'*The House Beautiful* is the play lousy.'

—Life

NOTES

All of the numbered quotes in this chapter come from *The Book of Theatre Quotes* by Gordon Snell, Angus and Robertson, 1982 [referred to in the notes below as *Quotes*].

1 *Quotes*, p. 97
2 *Quotes*, p. 97
3 *Quotes*, p. 97
4 *Quotes*, p. 97
5 *Quotes*, p. 5
6 *Quotes*, p. 5

14
A DRAMATIC INTERLUDE

An interlude to be used somewhere in a night of drama that takes risks. Rather than allow the audience to be critics, the performers take the initiative and express what some of the audience may be thinking. The result should be complete confusion. Should fit well just before interval.

PLAY WITHIN A PLAY WITHIN A . . .

CHARACTERS

Audience member—A (real name)
Six actors B,C,D,E,F,G (real names)
The director
The stage manager
Lighting technician

A: I'm going [*stands*]. This is rubbish. In fact, I want my money back. [*to neighbour*] Can you believe this?
B: You can't have your money back. Now sit down and stop interrupting.
A: Why can't I have my money back?
B: Because . . . Well, it's like when you've had a bad meal at a restaurant.

A DRAMATIC INTERLUDE

A: You mean I feel sick.
B: No, the time to ask for your money back is before you eat.
A: Well then, how will I know if it's bad?
B: It will make you sick?
A: No. How will I know if it's bad before I've eaten it.
B: Oh! You'll know that, surely.
A: OK, then. I feel sick. I want my money back.
B: Where did you eat tonight?
A: Not sick in the stomach; sick in the head.
B: I'm sorry.
A: You should be sorry; it's your fault.
B: Sorry?
A: This . . . it's your fault.
B: How can it be my fault; I'm an actor. I haven't been to a restaurant for years—unlike many I can see here in the audience.
A: It's not the restaurant, it's the play.
B: What is?
A: This is. This . . . is the play.
B: Is it? I thought this . . . was a complaint.
A: It is a complaint—about the play.
B: But to everyone else, this complaint is the play.
A: Can't I please just have my money?
B: I thought I'd already explained.
A: What has the restaurant got to do with anything?
B: You've already had your meal, so to speak.
A: What do you mean . . . meal?
B: You've already seen the play; there's no point asking for your money back.
A: Ah, but it isn't finished yet. It's still going.
B: [*pause, thinks*] Yes it is, this . . . ah . . . is the end of the last scene.
A: But we haven't finished yet.
B: Yes we have; or we will have if you leave to collect your money.
A: No, listen to us; we're still talking.
B: Not for long! Now ladies and gentlemen, wasn't that fascinating? Thank you all for coming this evening. You'll find that there is coffee . . .
A: [*coming down on stage*] No! No! Sit down, everyone.
  [*clapping*] Stop that applause.
C: But it's finished.
A: We're far from finished. We've got lots of talking to do.
C: I'm going. [*stands*] This is rubbish! In fact, I want my money back.
  [*to neighbour*] Can you believe this?
A: Sit down! You're just confusing things.
C: But that's my line. I have to say my lines.
A: So you're acting; you don't really want your money back?

C: Well, thanks a lot; they're [*audience*] not supposed to know that!
A: Sorry.
C: And, if you don't mind, you've stolen most of my lines already. If we can just get on with the play . . . I want my money back!
A: Sit down! [*does so*] Look, this show's obviously far from over. Can't I just have my money back?
B: I'll tell you what I'll do. The problem in the restaurant . . .
A: Restaurant again!
B: The problem in a restaurant is that you can't throw the food up again . . . can you?
A: Unless it's bad.
B: Yes, well, obviously unless it's bad. But you can't use the food again after it's been thrown up.
A: Unless it's a very bad restaurant.
B: If you've had your cake, you can't give it back.
A: You mean the performance.
B: Of course . . . what else? Unless you mean . . . .
A: No, no . . . the performance . . . exactly . . . I want my money back!
B: Well . . . Then we want our performance back!
A: But you can't. You've already done it.
B: Ah . . . but it can be done again.
A: By who?!!
B: By you!
A: But I'm not an actor.
B: At this moment, neither am I.
C: But I am, now look here . . .
A: Sit down! [*sits*]
B: Well . . .
A: But I . . . I don't have a script.
C: Yes you do . . . you've got most of my lines, for a start.
A: But I'm not using a script.
C: Oh, so you're just improvising.
A: Yes, I mean, no.
C: You can't even remember your lines.
A: Sit down!
B: D [*real name*] have you been copying this down?
D: Every word! [*spotlight on audience member with clipboard*]
B: There, we've got a script.
D: [*coming on stage*] Here we are. One copy each and one [to C] for you.
C: None of this is in the script!
D: Of course it is. I've just written it. That's your (A) part there. You start with, 'I'm going. This is rubbish. In fact, I . . .'.
A: I know! I know! They're my words!

A DRAMATIC INTERLUDE

D: You don't have to bite my head off. I'm only the scriptwriter.
A: But you didn't write this. These are my words.
D: Don't be silly. They're part of my script.
A: But you've just copied down what I said.
D: Poetic licence.
A: Poet [*chokes*]? What . . .? [*gesture*]
D: E[*real name*], are you getting all this down?
E: [*writing in the audience*] Every word!
  'But you didn't write this. These are my words.
  Don't be silly. They're part of my script.
  But you've just copied down what I said.
  Poetic licence.
  Poet [*chokes*] What? [*gesture*].
  Are you getting all this down?'
F: [*stands, writing*] Every word!
B: Great stuff, hey? I can't wait to find out how it ends. And you said we'd finished.
A: No, I said . . .
D: Yes . . . ?
E: Yes . . . I said . . .
B: See . . . we've got hours yet.
A: Hours? Can't I just have my money back now, please?
B: Just as soon as we finish this scene. You owe us one.
A: Alright . . . but just to the end of this scene.
B: Of course . . . only . . . to the end of this scene.
Dir: How's it going?
A: Who's that?
B: This is our director.
A: Pleased to meet you.
Dir: Likewise, I'm sure.
B: Here's your script.
Dir: Thanks, now who's this—'Irate audience member?'
A: That's me.
Dir: No, I'm sorry . . . you won't do at all. You just lack that, *Je ne sais quoi.*
A: Look mate, I've got more *sais quoi* in my little finger than you've had hot dinners—I think.
Dir: Promising . . . but you're not the type.
A: I just . . .
Dir: Quiet . . . I'm thinking. There we are. [*giving out scripts*] Perfect casting. Wait till you see this! It's going to be brilliant—absolutely brilliant.
A: But this says, 'Actor standing centre stage'. I'm supposed to be 'Irate audience member'.
Dir: Who's directing this . . . you or me?

A: Well, you . . . but . . .
Dir: [*putting arm around A's shoulder and walking around*] Now look [*searching*] ahh . . . . .
A: [*Real name*]
Dir: A [*name*], I don't want to hurt your feelings, but you're just nothing like an irate audience member. In fear of being accused of type casting I see you as the 'actor' type'. The straight honest performer desperately defending the shreds of his reputation and professionalism from this Phillistine in the audience. This oaf, this ill-mannered . . .
A: OK, OK, let's just get it over with.
Dir: Positions everyone.
[*B rushes into the audience*]
[*A confused*]
You just stay there.
Action!
B: I'm going, this is rubbish! In fact, I want my money back.
A: [*reading badly*] You can't have your money back. Now, sit down and stop interrupting.
Dir: Sorry, can we just hold it there, ah . . .?
A: A [*name*]
Dir: A [*name*] That was . . . awful. I'm sorry. I know I shouldn't say that, but I know that you will appreciate my honesty. Now . . . ah . . . .
A: [*name*]
Dir: A [*name*], you are a professional; an actor. You've just spent months putting this show together and this . . . this . . . this pig-ignorant piece of . . .
A: Theatrical garbage!
Dir: That's the spirit. This . . . thing is questioning the very basis of your existence—your creativity itself.
A: [*warming*] Animal . . . mongrel! . . . how dare . . .
G: Now, we're getting somewhere.
SM: [*with headsets*] Excuse me, but I've run out of cues.
Dir: [*searching the script*] I can't find that line anywhere.
LX: [*from the lighting box, if possible*] There aren't any more cues. What do we do now?
Dir: [*searching*] Have I lost my place?
G: This is rubbish! I want my money back.
A: Sit down and enjoy the show. Stand up again and I'll belt you one!
Dir: Fabulous! Stanislavskyish! Pinteresque! Brechtian gone bonkers! Motivation combined with alienation. They're going to love you on opening night. Break everybody!
[*everyone, including audience plants, leave, congratulating A and each other on fine performances. A is left*]

B: Coming?
A: Why not?
 [*Throws the script over his shoulder and leaves. Returns to retrieve the script. Reads*] Wait for me . . . [*runs out*]
 Houselights up.